A Collection of interesting encou

A Collection of interesting encounters with cryptids 1

An Encounter with a Bigfoot

This is a story of some kind, one could say. An experience of trust and intuition. It was early spring and winter had just faded away into another slumber. The sky was blue with some clouds covering a part of its prowess. There was something in the morning air, which was enticing, but one could not exactly tell, what it was. Was it the fact, that spring was invading nature for another time until summer would appear in its full bloom?

Who should know and who would care, but some guy, who loved to hang out in the woods of Oregon near the border to the state of Washington. How he loved to enjoy the darkness vanishing into the first rays of light, which always were some sign of relief or maybe a kind of refuge? Who could tell, what it was, but some old chief of the Haida clan, which used to roam the forests. The forests, which were part of the great hairy man, who had been visiting it for ages. The Indians believed in the myths, the legends of the Sasquatch and believed, that it was a human species, some kind of old human from ancient yore and lore. The guy, the hero of this story, if one wants to express it in this kind of manner, was a loner, a ranger dreaming of the great wide open, a cowboy, who loved nature and its beauty. To him, everything was just a miracle, an expression of art, which always showed a new aspect of itself. An aspect, which would prove to him it's seeming endless power and magnificence. And this was the reason why Perry, the protagonist of this story, was hanging out a lot in nature because he always could discover something new.

„This day will be another great day." Perry thought, whilst wandering through the forest again. The moon was crescent and the trees were illuminated by its rays. Perry could feel the cold of the night, which was waning, but this time it was different, this time there was some presence surrounding him, which he normally didn't feel. The Indians said, that one could feel the sasquatch when it walks, and that some of its kind would purvey some kind of coolness, which could be described as a soft chilly wind. This is what Perry could feel, while he was thinking about the legends of the Indians and the ancient tribe of the hairy people, which were supposedly visiting the forests of this part of Oregon.

Perry knew the hiking trails quite well and never really believed the tales of this ancient tribe, which normal folks would dub the „Bigfoot". But now, he really could perceive a presence watching him, following him through the forests. This notion of having the possibility, that someone or something was observing his every move, was quite frightening to him, because of his frail mind, which had already experienced a lot of query experiences starting with his infancy. It was amazing, that he reached the age, that he had reached because he already had had many moments, where he wanted to end his life. The hardships of growing up in a home of tears and the death of his wife Meredith had been too much for his weak and tender soul.

There was just so much damage and garbage, which from time to time would just engulf his mind with worries and plight. This is also a reason why he had to escape from it all and just be a part of a greater experience, untouched from man. To him this wandering through the forests was or could be described as a kind of therapeutical method, to cope with his cumbersome life. A life, that he wanted to forget and just leave behind like dust in the wind. Perry could hear the branches of the trees brake and the thumping of footsteps, but they were no footsteps of an ordinary animal, that he had ever heard. „Could this be just the wind, whipping up the branches or maybe a bear lost at the end of the night?"

Perry thought, ascertaining, that it just could not be a sasquatch, a being considered to be a mere myth. Why should he believe something like this to be true? „My mind must be playing tricks on me. Perhaps I am just too jaded and bewildered." he pondered strongly. But then he heard the footsteps again and again. Perry decided to walk faster and wanted to head to a cabin, where he could reassess the situation. The cabin was not very far, but he was nervous, not knowing, what was going on.

Then he shuddered for a second, a penetrating roar, coming from behind penetrated his mind. Perry kept on walking, but then all of a sudden, a figure of a hairy thing appeared in front of the path. "What is this, is it an animal or something else?" Perry thought to himself. The figure watched him and just stood there. Perry was completely startled and froze. Now he was confronted with something, that he really could not comprehend, something, that was massive and probably dangerous. Why was it here? What did it want from him? Was it a bigfoot? So, the legends had some truth to them and the Indians were not lying? All these questions were popping through his mind like a storm of unprecedented velocity. This could just not be true. This was not happening. Then the creature came towards him and he could feel its presence getting stronger and stronger. Then the creature stopped a few feet in front of him. The eyes of the creature had a yellow tinge and its facial features resembled a human, although it was covered in a brownish fur. "What are you looking for?" it asked in a growling tone. It could speak, it really could communicate with him? This was incredible. But what should he say now? What should he do? So, Perry decided to answer diplomatically: "I am just hiking, I like to wander in these forests. I mean you no harm, I just love nature and all its beauty. I don't know who or what you are, but I am not looking for trouble."

The creature groaned and growled and then it spoke: "Are you looking for us? Do you want to know us and our ways?" Perry stared at the creature and was petrified. What did it mean with the words, that it just said? Was it a trick, some sort of hoax or a did it want to ask him something? Why should he look for a bigfoot if he did not believe in them in the first place, the whole concept of looking for them was ludicrous or did he unconsciously yearn to see them? Then he remembered, that he did believe in them when he was younger and not so caught up in the world, which denied everything, that did not fit its concept, it's ideas. Perry answered with a frightened tone: "Yes, perhaps I was unconsciously looking for you. Perhaps I wanted to know, that you existed and that you were not some figment of an old Indians imagination." The bigfoot started to chuckle and responded in a friendly tone: "So now you are being honest, now you are telling the truth. Beware, we can sense deceit for a mile. You should open your mind and speak from your heart, where your desires lie. Most people, who wander hear are full of hate and anger and that is why we have to protect the forests from them. You must know, that we are the keepers of these lands and we don't like people who treat them with disrespect. We want people to love nature and respect its beauty and we want them to leave us alone. This is the reason why we avoid humans because most of them are so immature and hateful."

Perry listened to what the bigfoot had said and thought of what he could say next, but he was still quite confused. Then he decided to say these words of honesty to the bigfoot: "Yes, what you are saying is the truth, but I am not like these humans. I mean you no harm and I want to respect nature and your people if you are people I mean. At least according to the Indians, you are a kind of people, but I just want to express to you, that I do feel a lot of gratitude towards nature and its endless variations. I also respect these forests and your ways, even if they are different from mine." The bigfoot sighed and went taciturn for a while and then it said: "I understand, you are being honest and I respect Your thoughts, let me show you something of our world and let me show you, that we are good and kind people, who just, as I mentioned before, want to preserve nature's beauty." After saying these sentences the bigfoot backed off and gave him a sign to follow it. Perry hesitated at first and then he followed it off the path into the forest. The bigfoot leads him through parts of the forests, which were quite unknown to him. After following it for about 10 minutes he could hearken the sound of water flowing. Perry thought to himself, that they must be near some small creek, which he, by the way, did not know because he never ventured into that part of the forest. The bigfoot went on to the creek and stopped there, then it knelt and started to mumble something in some language, which Perry had never heard in his life. Perry waited behind it and patiently waited until it finished doing, whatever it was doing, for he could not exactly tell, what it was doing whilst mumbling and kneeling.

After it had ceased doing whatever it was doing, it turned towards him and handed him some kind of gift. "Keep this as a souvenir, and let it bless your life with wisdom, care, and love. I must go now Perry and perhaps we may meet again someday, who knows. Maybe the winds and the trees know because they often know us better than we know ourselves, for we are also not perfect. May the light bless you Perry and till next time." After speaking these words, the bigfoot went away and disappeared into the depths of the forest. Soon Perry could not even hear the slightest sound of its thumping footsteps. This was a scary, but amazing experience, which he had never had in his life. Now he was changed and his mind seemed to have been renewed by this action. Perry decided to stay at the creek for a while and looked at the gift, which seemed to be wrapped in some kind of material, which he could not recognize. The sound of the water was so comforting to his mind, which still was in quite a haze and very bamboozled.

After a while though, he felt the urge to move on and head back to his car, which he left five miles down the path, which he had taken. Then he heard a voice speaking to his mind: "Go back to the path, which is at the right side of you. It is not very far, just a few hundred yards, so you don't have to worry about losing your way in the forest." Who was this voice and why did it know where the path was? This question was intriguing and riveting at the same time, but Perry listened to, what the voice had told him and kept to his right. After a few minutes, he could see the path, which he knew quite well, although he perceived it slightly differently this time. Something had changed, or was it him who had changed?

As he was walking on the path on the way back to his car, he began to ponder about the things, that occurred to him and he realized, that his perception about life and its endless variations had changed in a decisive way, but he was not sure how it really had happened, that change, that had taken place in himself. Was it the encounter with the bigfoot? Was it the magical creek? Or was it the present from the bigfoot, which he had tucked into his jacket? He didn't know, but the new experience the new self was a wonder to him and gave him a feeling of true freedom. Now he could feel nature the way he should have perceived it a long time ago, and as he arrived at his car, he could sense some form of peace surrounding him, enshrouding him. He stepped into his car and drove home back to his house, which was 20 miles away, but the joy was now his companion. He could see the first rays of the morning while he was driving and breathe the fresh air coming from his car window, which he had opened to some degree. After half an hour he had returned to his house and opened the gates of his front door. He unlocked the door of his house and went inside to his living room, where he sat down on his couch for a while. Amazement and peace encircled him and he unwrapped the gift. The gift was a shining talisman, which he then kept in a draw.

Now he finally was free from all his burdens, because he had learned a new way of seeing things, which were honesty and acceptance for everything that was and will be.

He smiled and was happy again after a long time of sorrow and grief. This would be the beginning of a new and more conscious life for him and that is what he was yearning for all along. So, the tales of the Indians were true and the bigfoot were the keepers of the forest, as he had realized after this encounter, which he had. Thankfully he said to himself: "Thank You for the gift, now I understand, what it is. Saying this and being changed he decided to write down his encounter with the bigfoot and tell the world, that they were alive and kicking and here to heal, not to destroy or kill. A kind of people, who just wanted to live in peace and inspire the ones, who were open-minded to do likewise. Perhaps everyone could learn from this experience he then thought, after writing down his experience with the bigfoot and smiled, whilst enjoying the brightness of this new day.

A day filled with gladness and hope for a new life to change things in the world for the better.

The End

A shorty story about the Moehau man: The New Zealand Bigfoot

Many legends and stories never cease to exist, when it comes to this creature, which supposedly is roaming the New Zealand Bush. The Maori even once revered this being and would not venture into the bush, where it was dwelling. This story is about an encounter with such a creature, a cryptid, that has not been well studied, because the land Aotearoa, as the Maoris call it, does not share a long history with man, therefore the knowledge about this specific cryptid, is not that great.

So, it is no wonder, that most people have never heard of its existence, let alone believe, that it is alive and kicking. But this story is a testimony of a man, who has had contact with such a gentle beast of unknown origin. It was an autumn day and according to Mr. Jack Jonstone, it must have been late September, when he had first seen this being, whom he could believe to exist until he had had this first-hand experience. The year when he had his first encounter was the year John F. Kennedy was assassinated and the somber message was felt throughout Aotearoa. Many people were mourning the death of such a man of exceptional qualities, albeit refined manners and high morals. Here is the story of his account:

I clearly can remember the day, it was sunny and perhaps a bit chilly at first, but then the warmth of the maritime breeze pervaded the air. I guess, that was driving to the bush to relax and just enjoy my lifestyle, which might in some regard be seen as a precursor to the hippie culture, which was yet to blossom. Well, I don't know how long I was driving, I just know, that I started in Wellington and maybe made one or two stops, whilst bearing in my mind, that I wanted to reach my destination in the late afternoon. Driving past the beautiful Tararua Forest Park, I decided to take a little detour, hopefully, to get some new impressions of the landscape, which sometimes seemed to enhance my creativity, which I needed for my profession. Oh, I think, that I haven't introduced myself yet. My name is Jack

Blent and I am a photographer and painter, who enjoys traveling the beautiful islands of New Zealand and the world, always trying to find something new to experience and discover, so that my horizon will never end expanding.

But let me now continue with my story, which is also of great interest, because of its extraordinary ending, although I now ascertain, that the Mocha man is a no more real myth because there have been several sightings in the last 40 years. Well, I was just on the way to the next forest park, wanting to check out the Rangiwahia hut, which lay in the Rhine forest; a beautiful and riveting forest full of charms of different origin. After a half an hour or so, I am not sure, I arrived at the park, after driving up past Tararua Forest Park, which is about 10 to 20 miles southwest of Ruahine Forest Park. I stopped my car after I had driven into the park and just relaxed for a moment or two when my pleasant solitude was silently disturbed by some movement coming from the near bush. At first, I thought, that it just might have been some pukeko or maybe some other bird. But after a while, after hearing various movements, which seemed to encircle the periphery of my surroundings, I came to the realization, that these noises these sounds, which were a mix of thumping footsteps and the brushing of twigs and shrubs, was caused by something more massive than a pukeko. Alone this notion, this whim perplexed and confused my mind, because I was aware, that we did not have any big bipedal mammals on this island. So, how could this even be possible, if it were supposed to be not possible? So, I went into a total mental haze and was feeling jaded in an instant, albeit mentally exhausted.

Then, curiosity betook me and I had the spontaneous idea of getting out of the car. I regret it now because looking back, it was a mistake. I looked around and they're not far from me I could see the image of a hairy being walking upright. I stared at the contours of this hairy being, which I was not able to recognize at that moment. Silence returned and for a while I was calm, but something forced me to walk into the park and see the prowess of its nature.

After perceiving my surroundings, I dared to venture deeper into the park, by walking on the road, leaving my car behind. I did not know, that what I was about to experience would be real or at least real to me. How should I have known, that a thing such as the Moehau Man, which was also known under the name Maeroero, was as authentic as the Yowie of Australia? Well, time swept past and I had almost reached a hut, which was on a hill, I saw it again. Swooping past me in the bush this creature, which had a fur of auburn hue, seemed to Then as I came to the hut, something happened which I did not reckon with.

The creature suddenly appeared about 15 foot away from me. For a while it stood with a hunched back; staring, examining my every move and trying to know something about me, which I never could have thought of being relevant to me. It was as if this creature, who had great resemblance with a bigfoot or a Yowie, although it did look exactly like them, according to my current understanding and knowledge. Then the Moehauman, what I am going to call it from this point of my story, stood up straight and I was stunned for a minute, petrified by its sheer physical superiority, which impressed me. Probably I still was quite conditioned by society, but I guess, that a 10 or 11-foot tall creature would leave a mark on everyone;

especially if you are not a giant human being. Now it was clear to me, that I was in the presence of the Moehau man, a cryptid, not even known by most Kiwis, our slang word for New Zealander. And after the Moehau man had rectified its stature, to demonstrate to me, that it was here and I was trespassing its territory, it started to moan and then mumble something, which I could not understand.

"This was it." I thought. For how should I have known, that it was not hungry or at least not interested in me. After a while, it left as quickly as it had appeared. Shocked and amazed I spent an hour or two at the hut, not knowing, what I was going to do next. This haze and confusion of mind lingered until I finally held a grip of myself and returned to my car, watching every one of my steps. I started the motor of my car and sped off and was no in a trance, listening to some Rock 'n' Roll music.

I don't know how why the idea of heading up to Coromandel came to my mind, but somewhere I thought, that someone had told me, that some cryptids, who just looked like the one, albeit similar, whom I had just seen, were said to roam the bush of Coromandel. So, I drove for at least six or more hours, stopping in the Taupo on the way.

I was in a very odd state of mind and I ascertain, that I could have easily compared myself with the most extravagant hippie, who did not even see the light of day when I had this experience with the Moehau man in Ruahine State Park. Maybe it was even fate, which caused me to drive to Coromandel, where I would drive on the 25, which goes around most of the peninsula and even gives you a good view of the Coromandel State Park, which also inhabits Moehau men, which are the New Zealand version of the Bigfoot in America or the Yowie of Australia.

I am sure now, that I was searching for another experience with this Moehau man. I just wanted to find out more about it and it was this avidity, this thirst for more knowledge about it, which forced me to drive very vigilantly, always on the lookout, always hoping to see another one, but that did not happen, at least not, until the fall of night. So, after driving the whole 25 up and down two times, I decided to stay the night at an Inn, while I was driving on Tapu Coroglen Road, which I was so keen on driving on, because went straight across the Coromandel bush and that is probably the reason, why I was so impressed by this road. But I must add, that the wildlife and the flora are unique, even compared to most parts of New Zealand, because there are some plants and animals, which you can only find in this region.

I don't exactly know, where it occurred, my second encounter with the Moehau man, who can be as any other individual. Perhaps it even depends on how you are as a human being, because I opine, that such a creature is astute and reacts to your feelings, thoughts, and emotions, which probably most people, who encounter such a being, totally underestimate.

But to make a long story short, I was just about a few kilometers away from Coroglen, a little town, not far from the Coromandel State Park, when I saw the shadow of something big and furry. I immediately stopped my car and out of pure curiosity wanted to see, whether I would see the Moehau man again. A moment later the Moehau Man appeared out of the bush and just stared at my car. I froze and was petrified. The eyes of this creature were of a brown-reddish complexion and the light of the crescent moon perfectly depicted the outlines and the figure of this impressive Moehau Man. It was amazing to see it, and I did not dare to get out of the car. Suddenly I thought, that I had heard a voice speaking to me and I realized, that it was the creature, which was about 10 meters away from me. It said in a rude tone: "You better leave now or else I will have to harm you. My kind does not like people, who study it. For a long time, we have been living here and we want to keep it that way. Do you understand human?" the Moehau man spoke so clearly and loudly, that I was baffled, for I could not fathom, that such a creature had the capability of talking, let alone know what I was doing. I pulled down the window of my car and yelled: "Okay. I will not bother you or your kind. I am just amazed, that you exist and that the tales are true." Then I started my machine and drove off to the next Hotel, where I was greeted oddly.

As I asked the female receptionist, if she had heard of any stories of the New Zealand Bigfoot, the Moehau Man, she just burst out into laughter and said: "You must be joking right? Such a thing as a hairy creature does not exist. What are you on?"

I just ignored the woman's sheer ignorance concerning the matter and booked a room for the night. As I went to sleep though, I thought, that I could hear sounds coming from the nearby bush. Was it a Moehau Man wandering through the night or was I just imaging something again? Well, everything which I have experienced his true and hard to digest for some people, who probably never think about life and its purpose; but here it is my story of the Moehau Man, a subject so clandestine for most, that they won't even dare to address it.

Take the information or leave it. Think what you will, I don't care, I know what I have seen and it was not a normal animal. This New Zealand Bigfoot is a bipedal being and it is very sagacious and ferocious, so you better think twice, if you venture out alone in the bush at night, for the Moehau man is alive and kicking and not only has been seen on the North Island but on the South Island too.

So, this is the written riveting story of Mr. Jonstone, who has had first-hand experiences with the New Zealand Bigfoot, whom some call the Moehau Man or the

Maeroero Man, who has been living in Aotearoa for many centuries, long before the Maoris and the Europeans. This is his personal experience and I don't possibly share its content, but the real phenomenon of the Moehau man remains to this day.

The End

A story of eternity

The dark embers of a new day's light were about to encompass the sky. Still, silence and a frail silhouette were pervading the space of the outside world. The dark veil had not yet been lifted once again and a kind of chilly wind billowed above the old graveyard. The thoughts of life, which bestowed on to the thinkers, the poets, the artists, the men of aptitude, would once more succumb to the joy of intellectual perfection — even if they were only to taste the climax, the crest of utmost magnitude for on moment. Fear and iniquity were prevailing in the perplexed mind of our character. The character, which would play a role in this mere huge vast sea of incomprehensible being of life. The heist caused by dismal inspired minds, which ended up to become an immense energy heist, would soon be vanquished. Hope and joy would fulfill our characters life, as in his days of serendipity.

O yes, the cumbersome years were waning and a new man in Christ was hatching out of a grey and not so blessed butterfly-cocoon. The happiness, the agape love of the holy spirit was overflowing and almost drowning him in the purest love of parahyperinfinite source. The juggernaut of burdens, which had a huge impact on the past, of our subject, seemed to be disappearing, as he wandered through the mist of the cold and damp forest. The forest of queer conceptions, which no one dared to venture alone, especially at night and when it was bare of sunlight.

The forests, as the ancient keepers once told, were full of creatures, and not all of these were of friendly psychological concoction. Some of them, so one of the old keepers said: were evil and far from love and compassion. Rumors had it, that the forests were infested with secret portals, which like a window to a different time and place, would offer someone in a frenzy some sort of solace, lest he knew what he was doing and could deal with the other time and world, which most human minds refuse to accept as a given reality of its own individual distinguished existence. Who would dare to refute this incredible thought of truth anyway?

I guess, that only a valiant mind of hard and stark spirit could rebuke this thesis of other worlds, but just logical argumentation the thesis of them existing as much more probable, than them just being the figment of some frantic writers imagination, albeit hard to prove with common means. So the figure of this story was well on his way to the chapel of stone, which was a good three miles into the forest, not far from the old pine creek, which ran into the town of Newerslokburg, Ontario.

The shades of fall were already visible and the leaves were turning into a wonderful spectrum of colors. A new day was just about to protrude the trees with its first birth pangs of light, when something, some noise of ancient time, some thumping made the plants shiver with trembling fright. What was this unearthly sound? Where did it come from? Was it just a whim of vivid phantasy or some autosuggestive automatic unconscious created perception of the human mind? Alas ascertaining, that in a world of seeming logic it should be merely a fictitious thing, an imaginary hallucination of no importance. But what is logic anyway, but a mere word, a mere thought of man expressed in letters. The sound arose again and this time it pervaded the air and all its surroundings. Thumping on the trodden path of old yokes stead could be heard now for a good hundred yards. What on earth was this? Have there not been similar stories told by the old tribe of the Cree, Ojibwa, Algonkin or Spokane. Then a weird cracking of the branches followed, and the strange thing about it was, that the cracks were happening at a very unusual velocity rate. Especially the intervals between the cracks were waning by every sound, that was made. Then for a moment, which could in itself be described as an eternity in its own right, there was silence. Silene, which was accompanied by her sweet sister's tranquility and ease.

The world will never know, what does reside in every forest every place, that we call earth. What is intrepid thought, what is its goal? Who should know, but the wise old Indian, whom I called my friend, a guy, who had been wandering through the forest now for many decades? A peaceful guy of 85 years and full of life and joy. So much light and happiness were in him, and everyone, whom he met, had respect for him and his ways. He knew the ways of the old tribes and paid respect to the old legend of the sasquatch, which roamed the forests of America for thousands of years. He knew it's passions and it's weaknesses and was always attuned with the forest and it's a variety of species and spiritual beings, which his tribe called ghosts or sprites of yonder. The sasquatch were something in between, according to the legends of his tribe, which was older than the tribes mentioned above. His tribe had been here before the Cree, Ojibwa, Algonkin, and Spokane.

The old man by the name of Nkosi, an old Seminole name for a bear, had encountered many Sasquatch, but this time it would be an encounter of a different kind. This time he would meet a creature, which even to him would be veiled in mystery. The day Nokosi would come across upon this creature, which he thought to be a bigfoot, was a late day in October, the 28th to be exact. This day was started quite chilly and all the mirth of fall and its beautiful looming lush of autumnal colors seemed to be gone. Nkosi decided to drive to a forest near his place, which he had not seen, since his childhood days. Tension and a form of nervousness pervaded his state of being, which normally was governed by a stable, albeit calm mind. This day though was an exception to the rule and it contained its good share of quirks exempt from the usual perks and ups and downs, which most of Nokosi's days entailed.

As Nkosi got into his old rusty convertible, after he had drunk a cup of black coffee with some almond milk, which he normally would make himself, he noticed, that there was something about his convertible, which was not like it was supposed to be. The strange thing was, that he could perceive, that there was something wrong with it, but he could not find out what. As he turned on the engine of his car, everything seemed to be fine, but still, there was something about the sound of the engine which foretold, that the engine was not really in the best state and something was not quite right about it.

The drive to the forest was about a good half hour and it went smoothly if one did not include the bumps on the old and ragged road, which had seen better days. When Nokosi arrived at the place, where he wanted to do some hiking, he was a bit tired, maybe it was just a mere sign of his decrepitude and the hardships of life, which were telling him, that he was soon to pass away into the land, were his kin had gone to before him? Who knows? As he stepped out of his Convertible he took a deep breath of the fresh air, which was filled with a lush green and beauty of nature, as it had been centuries before. Something about this place was special and it was not only the fact, that his ancestors had their burial grounds there, but something else perhaps the fact, that it was some kind of twilight zone, where worlds collided, worlds of unknown grace and origin.

Nkosi took his backpack out of the car's trunk and locked it. He then locked the doors of his car and started his hike. But before he commenced walking, he stood in awe for a while and said a prayer in his native tongue, the tongue of the Seminole tribe.

Then his journey started, which would lead him deep into the forest and the mountains, which lay beyond. Nkosi gently strode on the trail, carefully observing every step he made and always took a short glance at every tree, he passed. It would not take long until he heard some weird sounds, which were not the usual sound caused by a squirrel, mink, bear or cougar. Nkosi, although he was aware, that he may be in the proximity of a Sasquatch, continued to hike on the trail and said the words: "One enhance."; which meant: "I am a friend!".

Then suddenly Nokosi could see a vague image of a being walking behind some tall cedar trees. The being slowly came towards him and now Nokosi could see, that it was some kind of Sasquatch, in spite of its different facial appearance and its slightly diverse build, which made it unique to him.

Nkosi stopped walking and just stood there, waiting to greet the creature, who was now very close to him, slowly approaching him with a soft and subtle stride. As the being, this Sasquatch, who was not really a Sasquatch, but something different, was only about 10 feet away from Nokosi, it stopped and stared into the old man's weary eyes, which could tell a big story of his life, which had seen and had its share of shadows, doubts, injustice, and anguish. "You are good! I can sense this! What are you searching for Seminole man?" the Sasquatch-like-being asked him in a deep tone, which seemed to resemble a bit of a bear's groan.

Nkosi looked at the creature which had a light brown hide and eyes of a human and a face which was similar to that of a Sasquatch and that of another creature, which he could not think of. "I guess, that I am just trying to find some peace and solace here for my troubled mind. This land here is the land of my people, who have been tested a lot by fate, but I think, that I don't have to tell you this because you know this already.

Perhaps I am also trying to understand something more about life, its essence, and purpose and why the Great Spirit has made it the way it is.

"That is good Nkosi! That is very good, the Great Spirit is everywhere and there is nothing in this reality, which is apart from it. I can tell you some of its mysteries, if you like, Nokosi?" the creature said speaking very softly, but still in a very deep voice. Nkosi was baffled, for he did not expect this being to be so intelligent, although he was aware, that some Sasquatch, albeit many, could speak. But the way the creature spoke to him and the fact, that it knew his name, astounded him." "Yes, okay. But first I would like to know who you are? You are not a Sasquatch, although you do share some common traits with it." Nkosi replied slightly agitated.

"Good, I will tell you who I am and then I will explain to you some things, which might enlighten or even rejuvenate and assuage your encumbered mind. I am a Sosok, a being, which comes from a different reality and place. I am related to some Sasquatch species roaming the lands of this country, but I am much more evolved and can easily think and learn in every form possible. I abhor every kind of intolerance and only love is my aim and the sole purpose of my existence. This might sound strange to you, but that is the way I am. And of course, I must add, that some Sasquatch are also similar to me in this respect."

Nkosi was awestruck, and he did not know what to say, realizing, that he was in the presence of something extremely unique and new to him.

"Very interesting and compelling. Perhaps you would like to tell me a bit more about you Sosok? How does your world look like? How many genders does your species have?" Nkosi asked still confused by the whole situation, which did not seem to master, albeit take some time to accommodate to. Sokos looked at Nokosi with his blue eyes and made a few steps towards him, after stopping about three feet away from him.

"Good, I will satisfy your thirst. I will quench your curious answers, which might sound strange to me, but I am used to a lot because a lot of folks out here have mistaken me for a Sasquatch. Well, let me begin with myself. I am a creature which we call Nukusa, which would translate as "forest traveler and adviser". I am very old and I usually don't count my age, because I was formed and spawned as an ageless creature, which can transcend time, which of course some Sasquatch can do too, but not to that degree like us Nukusa. So I hope, that your first question has been now answered to your satisfaction. Or would you like me to share some individual experiences, which I have had the past years? Or should I know to tell you something about the anatomy and attributes of my species?" Sokos asked with an ambiguous tone in his voice.

Nkosi looked at Sokos, who was now standing near him with his total prowess and stature, which was at least 12 feet, then he began to think and said: "Well, maybe you could just answer the second question first and then expound upon some of your individual experiences, which might be of interest to me."

"Okay. My species consists of three genders. We have a male, female and neutral sex. The third sex is rather a rare phenomenon amongst our species, but it still does appear now and then, although I must add, that we had many more members of the third sex, but that was a long time ago, long before this earth even existed. But I guess, this another story, which I rather would not prefer to share with you right now, because I still have something on my schedule; I am a busy Nukusa, you know. And now I will explain to you some things about our anatomy. Well, our anatomy is less dense than yours or other humans. We can adapt to every life form we see, that means, that we can change into every life form if we wish too.

And this reminds me of a very interesting experience, which I have had about ten years ago, not very far from here actually. So, let me start with this little story. I think it was at the beginning of your week because I must add, that we have a different calendar as you folks do, primarily because time does not play any big role in our society and our world in general. Well, I was walking through the forests of the mountains, which are five to ten miles from here. I was just inhaling the gentle and succulent fresh air of the mountains, as I saw a hiker, who seemed to have a very awkward behavioral conduct. It did not take a very long time until he could perceive me and at first, he was shocked until I told him in plain English: "Hey, it is okay. I am just another being, who means no harm to anyone.

My name is Sokos and yours!" It took this hiker about two minutes to respond. The first response was a bit harsh, so I decided to turn myself into a human man, who was about 6 foot 10 and that seemed to work. The hiker was still baffled and bamboozled, as he realized, that I had just transformed my body into a male human one. But then the conversation went smoothly and he was impressed, that I was capable of doing these things and could not really believe, that I was from a different reality; probably this has to do with the fact, that most human beings are so conditioned and indoctrinated, and also tend to have a very vertical horizon, which thwarts them to envisage another reality of which there are galore. And then after about half an hour, I bade him farewell and left. Well, this was one of my numerous encounters, which I have had, which was quite funny in a way, if I reminisce about it."

Sokos explained.

Nkosi was amazed at all the things, which he had just heard and could not grasp the fact, that he was in the presence of such a versatile being, which was much more than just a Sukusa. "Well, as I already have mentioned before, perhaps you would like to share one or two more interesting encounters, which you have had with my kind, albeit another one?" Nkosi replied, not really knowing what he should say, because the presence, the nighness of this being, had begun to alter his perception of the world and its reality, which at first made him scared, because he as well, like most mere mortals, had been traumatized, conditioned by the society, indoctrinated by the education system and his mental boundaries.

A moment of silence enshrouded Nokosi and Sokos and after this moment, this instant in time of peace and placidity had passed, Sokos commenced to respond: "Yes, I can share two encounters if you like? I mean I could even share three, it depends on your time of course? So, shall it be two more stories or three, you should decide dear Nokosi?"

Nkosi thought for a while and then after a minute of contemplating, concluded: "I guess, that the three stories if they are not too long, would be nice." Sokos eyes, which took on a somber tone, stared at Nokosi for a moment, amidst the quiet solitude, which now surrounded both of them and then he said quietly and full of reason: "Good, so three stories it shall be. The first of the three stories, which I will now share, occurred in the nineteenth century. I think it must have been at the end of it, but I am not too sure now, for I tend to forget the dates, because I constantly am having so many experiences, although I must stress, that this one was one of a kind. It was fall and the trees changed their colors into a beautiful spectrum of gold, brown and olive hue. The day was warm and beauty had the touch of serenity. I love these days, especially when they have something foretelling, something, which gives hope. Well, on this day, I believe it must have been the 15th of October, I was wandering through the Clear Creek State Forest, where I had been many times before. As I was roaming around and analyzing the trees; something I tend to do, when I walk through the forests, I saw someone or better-said something. For a moment I thought, that I was hallucinating because what I saw, did not fit the picture of a human. I decided to approach this dismal looking figure, which was lying on the ground, whimpering. The moment I had reached this creature, I realized, that it was a human, who was ghastly disfigured and full of anguish. Calmly and gentle I said: "Hello, I am a friend. Can I be of any help?" The person, a young girl, maybe 12 years of age or a bit older, replied in a whiny and sad voice: "No, no one can help me. I have been abandoned by my folks and they say, that I am of the devil." "Why should they say such a thing? Just because of the way you look? Just because of your appearance?" The girl raised her head and just gazed at me, perceiving that I too was a very odd figure, an odd creature. My stature or my physical appearance did not seem to intimidate her in any way and she said: "Well, I think, that I am not the only freak here. Mama and Papa cast me out of their home and I have been left her to die. This world is not for me and I don't know what I am going to do." I pitied the girl, who had been impaired by a spontaneous mutation of nature or God's whim. Pondering about how I could help her I spoke these words, which come so vividly to me, when I reiterate them: "If you like, you can come with me, into my world, where you will find acceptance, love, and joy." The girl commenced to cry again and blurted out: "Really? Really?" "Yes, I promise you, that my world has all these attributes and many more," I responded. "Okay. Then I'll go with you. Can you show it to me now?" the girl said, this time in a happier tone. "Yes. We can go now if you like?"

I added and the girl nodded. So, I opened a portal, picked her up and traveled through it into my world, where she now resides as an eternal being, who has no sign of mutation or mutilation whatsoever.

Hence this is the first story, which I have just told you; I must admit though, that it was the short version because the other two are a bit longer.

The second story was actually around 1900 and it happened in Michigan, which was at that time a quite interesting, but dangerous place, because of a lot of occult practices.

I was walking past a house, I actually have forgotten its name, which is not usual for me, because I normally remember every name. It was after dusk and I could feel an uncanny atmosphere surrounding it. Then suddenly I thought, that I had hearkened a scream coming from the house, which made me stumble and I decided to check out the house, which was a real manor house, one of these built around 1850 or so. So, I quickly teleported myself in front of the porch of the house and looked at its windows, which all seemed to be lit. Then I changed my form into a human, a Caucasian male, who could have been in his late forties. Then slowly went around the big house, which actually gave me a query feeling, because there was some dark presence, which made me feel really uncomfortable.

Then I heard another cry, which made me freeze for a second or two. And then a weird-looking figure peeked out of one of the windows. I think it must have been some sort of humanoid reptile, but I am not too sure, because it was too dark, to see a perfect image of this figure. Quickly I opted to make myself invisible and teleported myself inside, where I could hear very strange chanting, that was of a very evil manner. I went through the huge hallway and sped up the stairs, were I intuitively could sense where the chanting was coming from. The chanting was emanating from a room, which was guarded by some very tough looking guys, who seemed to have no remorse and would easily kill someone without wincing. I changed back into my real form and made myself visible to these guards, who were so shocked by my sudden appearance, that they fled the house. Then I opened the door and could see, that there were at least 20 people, who looked like lizards, chanting and just about to sacrifice another child, which was lying next to two freshly slaughtered children, which were ghastly mutilated, probably by these people or should I call them beings.

I gave my loudest roar, which drew their attention towards me, because they were in such a trance, that they did not even notice me entering the room. They glared at me hatefully and started hissing. Then they attacked me, but I managed to knock them all out. After I had done that I took the three of the five babies, who were still living with me. I did this by opening a portal and getting a big basket from my home, which is not far from my portal. Then I put the babies inside the basket and disappeared with them in my world. Later of course, perhaps a few weeks later, I gave them away to some good people, who were longing to have children, but could not have any.

So, this was the second story, now the last story, because I am noticing, that I am a bit short of time.

This story is probably the scariest one and happened in the early 30s. I was walking the streets of Chicago in a human form, to not be any sort of attraction and had the idea of visiting the Rosehill Cemetery, which to my knowledge is the biggest cemetery of Chicago. It was a rather cold day and soon it became dark as I ventured into the cemetery, which gave me some eerie sentiment of fear and remorse. Still, in my human form, I just was strolling through the big cemetery and looking at all the names of the deceased, who once dwelled on earth. My God have mercy upon their souls. Well, I think it must have been near that chapel, albeit a few hundred feet away as I saw a very tall figure of about 20 feet or more. It had sordid energy emanating from it, which scared me. I approached it carefully and wanted to know what it was doing. As I came closer, I noticed that it was hovering above the ground and somehow feeding of the energies, which surrounded the cemetery. Whilst doing that it was mumbling something in a very strange tongue, which I have never heard before in my life.

After a while, it realized that I was watching it. For a moment it just continued, what it probably had been doing for some time and then it suddenly appeared right in front of me and paralyzed me. I instantly changed my appearance and changed back into my original form. I roared and cried with all my might, but that did not seem to intimidate by any means.

I could not move nor think straight and that struck me with fear because I felt like a helpless victim, who was about to be devoured by such an evil thing, which I cannot describe to this day. This thing then dragged me to a place, which looked like a crypt. It hurled me inside and locked me in there.

Inside that crypt, I was confronted with total darkness and an evil presence, which was not that creature, but something else, which was lurking and feeding off my fears. The strange thing was, that I was neither able to telepathically contact any friendly creature in the proximity nor able to open a portal, this thing, whatever it was, just drained me of my capabilities and made me so weak, that I don't know how long I was locked in this crypt, but luckily, I think it must have been the next day. Someone opened the door and I was glad to see the light of day again.

The person, who opened the door was an old man, who was working in the cemetery during the daytime. Thankfully it was so dark, that he did not see my real me so that I had enough time to transform into a human; because who knows, how he would have reacted, if he had seen my real self? Well, that is it I guess and for now, I must leave you, because there are things, which I have to attend to. May the light bless you Nokosi and maybe until next time." After Sokos had told these three stories, as he had promised to Nokosi, he vanished right in front of Nokosi's eyes.

Nkosi was amazed by this whole experience with such a strange, but kind creature, that he stood on the path for a while until he decided to continue his hike, where he would enjoy the dusk on some mountain slope, staring at nature and the heritage of his tribe. But this encounter had changed his life's view to such an extent, that he from then on would just roam the forests of the United States, where he still could feel some vestige of the many Indian tribe's past, which may in the future, that was at least his hope, find some solace.

This is the story of Nkosi and his interaction with a bigfoot like being, who is much more than a bigfoot. Of course, one could discredit this account and disregard it as a mere concoction of phantasy, but who knows.

And who really can know, because the mystery of life is so great, that even the greatest minds have said, that they know, that they no nothing.

The End

A Dogman Encounter

Never venture into the woods, when it is dark, my mother told me, as I spent time with her on the farm. The farm was quite old, and it was a family relict, an heir of the pioneer era. Never walk alone in the forest, when the days look gloomy, because of it, the thing which many call a myth, a myth which has been haunting me all my life, until that day when it happened, when something occurred, that made my mind change, and changed a lot of doubt into fear and amazement.

Now I know why my mother warned me and why we heard some strange growls from time to time near our barn. There was always something eery about the farm and everyone who had the pleasure to visit it could perceive it. Even a strict atheist or a skeptic man or should I rather say a woman of science could feel something, that made it very odd. The reason for this will be expounded on in this story.

This story is the story of my encounter with something, that most mortals will renounce, will put into the realms of pure myth and legends, which are only the figment, a notion of human fantasy. But then again one should ask the question, what is fantasy, if not some kind of different reality, which does exist on some sort of plane, even if it is imagined by the human mind. But these questions are too philosophical for most human beings, who only perceive the world, the way the society wants them to think and perceive. Many people have flaunted and derided me for sharing this experience with you, you blessed reader, who dares to question the foundation the fundament of our reality and maybe has the courage to open his mind for new and other realities, which probably seem to exist or better formulated coexist with our reality, which and this I hold for a fact, has been conditioned by our society, which actually should be enlightened? But are we enlightened? Are we civilized? Well, these questions are so ambiguous and difficult to answer to a full extent. But these are just examples to convey my message, to prove to you reader, that this mythical creature called „dogman" is no product of my fantasy, but a real phenomenon. And to be honest with you reader I now must admit, that I never really believed in this myself, and this is my account, my testimony of something which will blow your mind and perhaps make you question everything. So, let me open the curtain and tell you my story of the dogman, which I had the pleasure to meet; perhaps I am being too sarcastic now, because in truth such a creature is no joke, no fairy tale, but a real thing, as I already have mentioned above.

So, let me commence to tell you my story which started on a rainy day in April or was it late March, well it doesn't matter. Let's settle on March and say, that it was raining, actually it was pouring buckets of water on to the old paved road to the farm of my parents. Many years had passed since I had seen them and I came there for one reason. This reason was the miserable health condition of my father, who was suffering from various acute diseases. Then I knew like some animals just feel things, which are going to happen, before they happen, well I guess you know, what I mean. I just knew that he would not linger in this place, we call earth for much longer. And this I don't mean in a judgemental way, but in an objective way of seeing and perceiving some things.

Well, perhaps I was just born with this gift of being able to sometimes see or feel things before they happened, in spite of thinking very materialistic at that stage of my life and wanting to see the world mainstream scientists wanted to see it. Well, it turned out that I was flawed, I was wrong, I didn't know anything about reality really and I was just too bold to admit that. But for now, I would like to return to my story, for this is the reason why I am writing this all down. Well, I was heading towards the farm from Madison, which was the town of my residence and the town of my kids and my wife. I decided to go alone, because I knew, that my parents could be a bit difficult to handle, especially in the state, that they both were in. Thus, I left my kids and my nice wife at home and took a trip, which should be the trip of my life to my parent's farm, which was quite far upstate. It was not quite too far away from Lake Superior, which was just a half-hour drive away from my parent's farm.

My parent's farm was quite large and a part of it was on an ancient Native American burial ground, which my family only discovered a century later. You must know, that the farm of my parents, was one of the first farms in that part of Wisconsin. And this is why it was so important for my parents, to always keep it in the family because it was or serves as a token for their work, their hard effort in a world, which is not always particularly bright or filled with kindness. The drive from Madison to the farm, which was in the upper part of the Northland, was quite a way. I decided to make a few stops and relax a bit at some random gas station. Everything went quite smooth, just that I could feel some weird presence surrounding me at some time. I think it was at the second gas station or so, that I felt the feeling you get when you know, that you are being watched, but don't know, who is watching you. This was that feeling that grew stronger, and now I must say by the mile. Really strange and still quite unexplainable to me now, but that is the way it seemed to me then and still seems to me now.

As if something or someone wanted to know something about me and followed me to the farm, which, when I arrived there had a creepy welcome. The barn and the house were still standing, but some strange cool wind was whistling around our house and our barn. The stables also had something eery to them, maybe it was because of the cloudy day and the cold rain, which lashed out on every unprotected pedestrian or in our case lonely wanderer, who made himself a little modest abode on our farm. You must know, that some homeless people and beggars wander the Northland of Wisconsin, seeking refuge and some warm hospitality, which the cold cities cannot give them anymore. Why this is so I can't tell, but it is a fact, that we have had our share of beggars and homeless people, whom we tried to help and gave some shelter for a good while. Kindness and hospitality were always the fundament of our family, which despite its flaws loved the lord and his mysterious ways.

As I stepped out of my car, I could feel some strange macabre cold, which had some unnatural attributes to it, which I cannot really explain, maybe it was just my imagination, but looking back it makes sense to me, because the legends say that the dogman has some kind of magic to it, which has a cold aura. I know, that this sounds quite crazy to someone, who has never experienced this, but to the believer, to the one, who has had an encounter with such a creature, can tell the tale of these strange occurrences, which happen, when it is nearby.

What the dogman is now one can tell and there are many theories, which try to explain it's the origin. But this is some complex matter, which I know don't want to touch upon. The door of our farmhouse seemed to be locked when I stood in front of it, which was very weird because normally my parents would leave it open. It was almost dusk, when I arrived and soon darkness would prevail again, gazing at the sky, which had some ominous signs, which I at that point could not understand, I decided to knock on the door and ring the doorbell, which was next to the door.

Awaited a while and saw how the lights lit up, as I felt something watching me again, the same feeling started to disperse in my body and soul, the same feeling I had at those two gas stations earlier on during my trip to the farm. After a while, a maiden by the name of Martha unlocked the door and opened it for me. She told me to come in swiftly and locked the door behind me.

As I asked her, why she locked the door, she told me, that some kind of animal was stalking the grounds of the farmland and had been seen by some workers last week.

„Excuse me, some animal, this sounds utterly ludicrous, there are no animals here, which could be of any danger. Besides they would never venture into our farm, because of our fences and our dogs." I said, looking at her with a serious expression on my face. „Well mister, you are mistaken, there is something out there, and it is more than an animal. Haven't you heard of the legends, the legends of that creature the..." I interrupted her quite harshly and said with a humoristic tone to my voice: „Yes, that story of that dog creature, come on, please. It doesn't exist, these are just fairy tales to scare little kids and keep them from wandering off at night. You know, that things such as this dogman, isn't it called that, don't exist. So just calm down and relax, there is nothing outside, just some nasty weather, that's all."

Martha stared at me and responded with a stark voice: „Well, if that is so then we can all sleep well tonight. You might know your city life, but out here many strange things occur, and frankly, I don't care, if you believe in them or not, I know, what I have seen and I have seen it." Many thoughts went through my mind and I just was in the mood for an argument with the woman and that is the reason why I just said: „Good for you, but I have not had to pleasure of meeting this creature, so please accept, that it is not very easy for me to believe in it. I hope you can pardon my ignorance concerning this matter and wish you a good night. Please let me see my parents though, I would just like to say hi before I'll go to sleep."

Martha smiled and lead me to their bedroom, which was located on the first floor, next to the flight of stairs, which also lead up to the second floor, where I would fall into a short slumber, because at that point I didn't have the faintest idea, of what would happen this night. I just could not imagine, that night could have so many surprises in store for such, at that time very narrow-minded and stubborn, a person like me. As I went up to the stairs, I thought, that I could hear a strange howl, which I didn't pay any real attention to. Martha heard it too, but did not comment it, because out of courtesy, she did not want to confront me with this dam dogman theme again, which from that moment on started to haunt my mind on some subconscious level.

As I opened the door to my parent's bedroom, it was very quiet, actually too quiet for my parents. My mother gave me a warm welcome and said in a calm voice: „Come on boy, take a sit. How was your trip?" „Good, I guess, and how are you and dad." I answered without really thinking of what I was saying because this kind of answers had been so often imprinted into my head, which had to do with my profession, where I always had to do this kind of small talk. „Your dad must be in the next room, he ain't feeling to well actually, it must have been another one of these nightmares about this human-looking dog." „Excuse me, did you just say human-dog, do you mean something like a dogman? Dad is having nightmares about a dogman? You must be kidding? Have you all lost your fricking mind? What do you all have with this dogman?" I responded with a quite interruptive tone. „I know, we know, that you don't believe in the dogman and you don't understand the way things are around here, but with some time, I hope, that you will comprehend, that we are not making these things up. There are many creatures out there and one of them is the dogman, which the french just to call „loup-garou", which means „werewolf" or „lycanthrope" in French. But it is more than a werewolf, it is something different, some of them are evil and some of them are good."

I could not understand what was going on, my mom was telling me theories about the dogman and my father was having nightmares, which contained the dogman. This was so surreal to me and I could not explain, what was happening, and on some level of my mind, I already could feel a certain unease and just knew, that something weird was really going on, but I could have never imagined, that it had the slightest to do with that creature, which still at that moment, was a made-up archetypical construct of human superstition. Confused I went into the room, where my dad was lying and breathing quietly.

An eery atmosphere could be sensed in the room and I said: „Hi dad, I'm here. I have justed arrived. How are you?"; to fill the atmosphere with some words, because this form of tranquility was giving me the creeps. My dad just moaned and then he whispered in my direction: „Have you seen it, son. Have you seen it? O my God, it is strong and fast. Watch out it, this dog thing is stalking our land."

Absolutely bamboozled about, what my dad had just uttered, a shudder surrounded my whole body and I all of a sudden had difficulties to breathe. I answered in a loud and earnest tone: „Everything is okay, dad. I am here and there is an explanation for what is going on here. Don't worry there is no dogman, it is just some fairy tale, invented by some old Indians, to scare off some stupid people. Come on dad, you don't believe this stuff, do you?" Then a moment of silence enshrouded me and him, and it was a very strange kind of silence, which had some uncanny aspects to it. Then I suddenly could hear another howl, but this time it was louder and clearer. „Do you hear it now son. This is what it does to scare its prey. It wants to sense the characteristics of its prey. Do you believe me now?" he spoke with an excited voice. „No dad, it is probably just a dog. Have a good night sleep. See you in the morning." I uttered back with a very calm voice.

As I went out the door to the room, where my mom was staying, I could hear him mumble: „Watch out boy, this ain't no dog, it is the dogman and he wants something. It is dogman son, watch out!" I closed the door behind him and could not understand, why he had said these words. „How delusional my father has become." I thought at that time, while I said another „Goodnight." to my mom, as I was heading out of my parent's bedroom and to the flight of stairs, which would lead me up to the second floor.

The instant I reached my room, which now was serving as a guest room, I could hear another howl, but this time it was longer and deeper. „Strange animal, this must be, I have never heard a howl like that." I thought to myself, as I opened the door of the room. The room was small and seemed very tidy as if no-one had been in it for a long time. The old chair and the desk were still at their usual place and the bed seemed to have some dust sprinkled on it. I just jumped on the bed and wanted to forget my trip and just talk about things in the morning. I was in no mood, for what was going to happen, because this, would be something which probably easily would surmount every kind of general thrill.

Luckily I could doze off a little and for a while, everything seemed fine, although, in reality, nothing was fine. As I went to sleep I found myself on the ground of my parent's farm. It was the hill, which was about a mile from my parent's house, which was where the forest started. I felt cold and the forest was exuding something mysterious, something terrifying. Suddenly I could hear something walking in the forest and watching me, observing me. I didn´t know what it was, but I froze for a second when I heard a large howling sound coming from it. Then eyes appeared out of the forest, red eyes staring right at me.

Now I could see the image of the hairy beast, which stood there beneath the trees for a second and then commenced to walk straight at me. It was a tall figure, at least 9 foot or so and it was walking on two legs. Canine features started to become visible and fangs, which must have been at least four inches big, protruding out of its upper jaw. It looked a bit like a lycanthrope, but something about it resembled some kind of dog, which had some human attributes to it. The creature, which could have been described as the dogman, was now right in front of me and snarled at me. Then it gave another really vicious howl, which penetrated my bones. Chills came down my spine and I turned away from it and ran as fast as I could. I could hear it following, keeping up my pace. A had the feeling, that it was playing with me because it could easily have just caught up with me and devoured me.

Then I woke up, totally sweating and full of fear. O just another nightmare I thought at this moment and just lay there on the bed of the room, where I was staying. But the nightmare was not just some nightmare, it was a really strange one because it was one about the dogman, who had been present for the last hours in every social interaction, that I had had. What a peculiar thing, that I just had a nightmare, where a dogman chased me on the property of my family. How weird was that, could this all be a coincidence, was my mind playing tricks on me. Why was my mother, my father, Martha so obsessed with that dogman theme? And the howls, where did they come from, they were really unusual, even for an animal. All these thoughts encompassed my mind and I didn't want to succumb to this blur of anxious thoughts, so I decided to go downstairs to the living room on the ground floor of my parent's manor house.

The moment I went down the stairs to the first floor, I could feel something strange, something intimidating, but decided to not submit my emotions to it. As I reached the ground floor, a could perceive extraordinary tranquility, even the clock was not ticking. Everything seemed quiet and peaceful. I went into the kitchen, to make myself some tea and stared through the opened door into the next room, which was an office leading to our closed veranda. The door to the closed veranda was open too and that was quite macabre because normally my parents would close the door of every room in the house.

For a split second, I thought, that I could see something at the window of the closed veranda. I thought that a saw some image, a shadow of something big in the distance, maybe, including the distance from the kitchen to the end of the veranda, 100 to 150 feet away from me. Again I thought, that my mind was playing tricks and I just boiled some water in one of our family kettles. A made myself some black tea, to wake up some more and stay up for the rest of the night.

Perhaps all these happenings had some logical solution and I was just imaging things because this just could not be true. As I finished making my tea and stepped into the living room, I could clearly hearken another howl, which seemed to be pretty close. I sat then on the couch and closed the door to the kitchen. Something was wrong and now I could feel it strongly, despite that I didn't pay any further attention to the howl and the following howls, which followed in intervals of different lengths. I just began to sip some of our finest black tea, which was actually homegrown.

I was just about to finish my wonderful cup of black tea, a shot was fired, then another one and another one, following the shots where ferocious growls and snarls, which lasted for about a minute or more. „Strange?" I thought, and lent back on the couch: „what was that?" I pondered, construing my own version of these events. At that time, as I am now, the shots must have been fired near our barn, but I had no clue, who had fired them. What was this person shooting at? Who was he or she, and what were his motives to do such a thing? The growls and snarls where they just coming from some angry dog? Or was it...? No, it couldn't be I thought to myself. „This just could not be real, this was all but a dream inside a dream, right Mr. Poe?" I thought to myself, completely distraught in some way or another.

A sense of fear surrounded me and my heart started pounding. After a while, I had the idea, which I would now consider as crazy or totally bonkers, to head outside with one of the rifles of my dad, which I took from the wardrobe, that was standing at the other side of our quite large living room. I grabbed some bullets inside a box, which were below the rifles. I must admit, that we had quite a lot of ammunition, because of some occurrences, which I don't want to expound upon now.

As I opened the door of our entrance, a cool breeze engulfed my body. It was quite chilly outside, but this breeze had some supernatural aspect to it. Slowly I wandered around the manor house, which had a very big basement, but two floors and an attic, which were a lot smaller, but still massive compared to a standard conventional floor of some ordinary sized home.

After I had passed the rear end of the left-wing of our manor house, I could hear something move near the barn. I loaded the rifle and aimed in the direction from where the movement probably came from. Then again I heard another sound, which resembled the sound of footsteps coming from the other side of the barn. What was going on? What was this? Could this be real? Something seemed to be circling the barn, something was out there lurking in the dark. I started heading towards the barn at a very slow pace and had a tight grip on the rifle, aiming at the dark veil of the cold night. As I almost had arrived at the barn I saw a pair of red eyes looking at me from the distance, staring at me with intrepid fervor.

The eyes must have been about 50 feet away from me and I could tell that they were behind one of our tall shrubs, which grew next to the barn. Was this thing, which had just moved around the house and the barn, at least be moving in the proximity of the house and the barn, hiding behind the shrub, to watch me, to study my strengths and weaknesses?

Then it happened the moment, which would change everything and everything, that I have ever learned and perceived in life, just vanished forever. The eyes moved and disappeared for a moment, only to appear in front of the shrub, which now gave me a clear vision of what I was dealing with. The red eyes were the eyes of a tall creature, which remarkably resembled the creature, this dogman of my nightmare. Its face was hairy, as it's the whole body. Its fur was of a brownish color, although I could not really tell, because of our weak lamps and the weak moonlight. It stood on two legs for sure and its face was very canine and there were fangs sticking out of its mouth.

The creature snarled at me and now it's huge snout appeared and now, there was no doubt in my mind, that this, what I was just witnessing, could only be the dogman. The dogman came closer towards me and I fired a shot, which made it whine but didn't stop it from coming closer. Then I fired two shots, which seemed to have at least streaked its body, but now I am sure, that I did not in any way injure the dogman.

The creature started howling with terrible strength, that I had never experienced in my life. Whilst it was howling wildly I started to run back to the manor house at full speed. Luckily the door was not locked, for that could have cost me my life because just after I had locked the entrance door of the manor house, the dogman lashed out at the door and smashed the window next to it.

The house was now alarmed and Martha ran out of her bedroom, which was in the basement and held a rifle in her hand. My mom, who was totally petrified came down the stairs with a Winchester gun and a Remington pistol. The dogman was now bashing the entrance door and Martha shot at fife times, out of the window, which it had totally smashed, but somehow realized, that it could not fit through it. I fired three more rounds at it myself and my mom fired all the rounds of her pistol and held the Winchester gun trembling with fear.

The dogman began to whine again and receded: I guess, that Martha must have hit one of its weak spots because it seemed to be wounded and finally vanished into the darkness. But who would know, that our fight with the dogman would last to the morning? Who would know, that this creature had the ability to quickly healing its wounds?

Who could tell, that it was looking for a weak spot in the manor house and, that it would not easily give up its prey, which was us? Totally exhausted from this horrible experience, I decided to sit in the living room with Martha, who told me, that she would be on guard and assist me if it should come again. My mom went back to her room, but chucked some bullets into a bag and grabbed at least three rifles. Fear and extreme unease pervaded the atmosphere of our home and now we all knew why. The dogman had been lurking out there and I, the fool, had not taken notice of all the warning signs, because of my stubbornness and my narrow-minded views.

How lucky I was, that I had survived the attack of a dogman, but still I had a feeling, that it was not over. Sipping on another cup of homegrown tea, I decided to figure out a good plan of how to successfully protect the manor house from such a beast of unknown origin. The battle for our home, the battle for our lives had now begun, or should I better say the war was now waging in us and the energies, which surrounded us. It would not be long until I dozed off, but only for a short while, because then I was torn out of my sleep and I could hear a howl, which was so terrible, that even my worst fiend should not hearken such a gruesome call, which could be described with a demonic manifestation out of a hellish place.

Then I heard the smashing of windows, I must have been windows on the first or second floor, but I was not really sure, because I was in a state of utter confusion and terror. I took my rifle and headed upstairs. Totally in awe, I saw, that the windows on the rear end of the floor in the hallway next to my parent's bedroom were totally demolished. Then something creepy happened, really eery. Something seemed to be moving around one of the rooms of that hallway, I think it was the former maiden room. I clearly could hear footsteps thumping on the wooden floor. Slowly I advanced to the place, where the odd noises were coming from.

There it stood the humungous beast, the dogman in the maiden room, which had it's door wide open. The room was large and there were a set of windows on its other side. The dogman seemed to be sniffing at the linen of the bed and held some underwear in ist right hand or should I better say claws. The dogman didn't stop sniffing for a while, although I am convinced, that it could feel my presence. I watched for some time, totally startled and petrified. Then it turned it's hairy snout and pair of cold red eyes towards me and growled.

As it leaped in my direction and swung its right arm towards me, I jumped aside and fired all the rounds I had. I guess, that some of them must have hit it because it commenced to whine again and fled crawling through the smashed windows or what was left of them. Martha appeared next to me and I was surprised, that she could sense the dogman very well, because the manor house, as I mentioned earlier, was not exactly little. I decided to go to my parent's bedroom and told them to lock the door and push some furniture against it.

The hours to the next sunrise were waning, but every minute seemed to me like an eternity. Now everything was out of balance and the paranormal or surreal was real. „Please light, please God, help me through this time of peril." I prayed. After doing that I returned to the living room and stayed there, while Martha held the guard in front of my parent's bedroom. Time was passing and it must have been early before dawn, when I heard some strange noises coming from upstairs, something was not right, so I grabbed some more bullets and went up the stairs, were Martha, whispered to me: „It is in the attic, the dogman is in the attic." „Okay, I'll finish this now. Come with me." I responded quietly.

Martha and I went up to the stairs to the second floor and then very slowly up to the attic, which was quite a challenge if you wanted to be unnoticed, because the stairs to the attic, were already quite brittle and tended to squeak if one stepped on them with normal speed and strength. As we reached the attic, walking on our tiptoes, we could see, that someone had turned on the lights. The attic was not very large and made up of four adjacent rooms. The first room was quiet and the sounds were definitely coming from the rear end of the attic.

We moved very slowly with our guns loaded. Every step we took, must have taken at least five seconds or more. As we reached the fourth room, we could see the dogman kneeling down and eating something. To my terror I realized, that it was the corpse of some man, maybe one of our workers and then I remembered the shots, that I had heard and my first encounter with the dogman. „Oh my god, I thought, this is too horrible to be true." I thought at that moment.

We, me and Martha went closer and could feel the movements it made and now I could finally see it's silvery-brownish fur. I decided to catch it's attention and yelled: „Hey dogman, it is time to leave this house. Either you go or we will be forced to shoot." The dogman immediately turned towards us and growled, then it whacked Martha so fast and strong, that she was on the floor. I receded a few steps back and fired all of my rounds, whilst taking out my pistol, which I had tucked into my jacket, which I had been wearing since my first encounter with the dogman.

The dogman was wounded and viciously attacked me with its claws, luckily I could dodge his attacks and had some time to fire six rounds of my pistol, which I aimed straight at its forehead. The dogman screamed, probably because it was seriously injured and jumped out of the windows at the horizontal end of the room. I could see how it ran into the darkness of the night and how it was hurrying into the nearby forest. I waited a while and felt relief, that I had never felt before. Soon the first rays of the sun gently caressed the sky.

The night vanished and a new day arose.

The dogman or I'll say this dogman never ever appeared on our property again. Thankfully we prayed and we all knew, that it must have been the grace of the power of the divine, the might of god, that spared our lives this night. Martha had survived the attack of the dogman, although she was severely injured and had to spend some time in the hospital. I decided to stay a few more days, so I could cope with the whole situation, because I didn't want to bother my wife and kids, with this experience of torment, fear, and horror.

But now it was over and this is my story, which might sound incredible to you, and actually, you are not forced to believe anything, that I told you. Just bear in mind, if you are out in the woods of Michigan, Wisconsin or even some parts of Canada and who knows were else, that there might be a creature out there, bigger and stronger, than you can or want to imagine, which witnesses have named the dogman.

The Dogman

I don't know who I should commence this very awkward story, which probably most won't believe, because they perhaps are not prepared to change their perception of reality. But this is what happened to me, and probably many others out there, who have lived to tell this tale, which one could consider as a creepy one. It was in late February when I drove out to my ranch, which was about 50 miles away from the City of Milwaukee. The city I really fancied quite a lot and I can also tell you why. Such splendor sprawled out next to the beautiful lake Michigan, which has some things to discover or better said be discovered.

Especially at dusk when the ray of the suns gives it that kind of pretty sparkle, that one is used to whilst glaring at a gem gleaming. Besides this gorgeous attribute of lake Michigan, which really does in a kind of way harmonize with the City Milwaukee.

There are many other things, which are teeming in its busy streets, roads and silent highways. Could you guess what I am trying to convey with that, well frankly I'll just say, what I wanted to say: the city is full of pretty people, nice girls and some queer intellectuals, who normally roam the city after dusk. Perhaps this is some kind of intellectual tradition, I don't know, but my experience tells me, that it must be that way because I have never ventured into a bar or someplace during the day and met a man of such caliber. So this said I want to return to my story, the experiences, which I had whilst driving to my ranch and which I actually then had on my ranch. But before I want to tell you, avid reader, more about my story I would really like to introduce myself and explain to you, so you maybe can comprehend where I am coming from and which walk of life I have experienced.

Well, I am a divorced man of 52 and I have two kids, a daughter, and a son. My wife went to Memphis, Tennessee and this is where some of my hardships start because of that I don't get to see my kids much. Actually, I am very glad when I get to see them every spring and every Christmas.

Well, that is a different story, but I think I still should mention these things, so understand, that I am not some weird loner crackpot making up silly stories to disturb your worried minds, which have to survive every day of life's many challenges. So I am 52 and I am by the way a studied man and have dedicated most of my life to science, biology, to be exact. Perhaps this will make it all the more riveting, who knows.

As I have already mentioned it was a late day in February and I had just decided to head up to my ranch, my farm, which I had actually purchased five years ago, because of various reasons. One reason was the anxious call of one of my rangers, who rang me two days ago and told me that he had found some of my cattle mutilated and dead. So this was the reason why I was going to my ranch, because of this occurrence and another strange event, which happened last fall, and still couldn't really be explained to my content.

Last fall some of my cattle went missing and then a few weeks later, bones where found, which later were analyzed in a lab. And do you know what the bizarre about this is?

Well, the bones turned out to match the DNA of my cattle. The bones where of the same breed as my cattle and actually were related with some of my cows. So this event and the anxious phone call forged the decision to check out my ranch. But I must admit, that the bones, which were found last fall and the mutilated dead cattle, gave me shivers down my spine.

What could have actually caused all this havoc and dismay? Was it just some lunatic? Or a very deranged animal, distressed and lost? Or what could it actually be? I mean I have heard of the phenomena of mutilated dead cattle before, but they were sometimes associated with alien abductions, especially these beings, which ufologists dubbed „the greys", but that could not be the case here or not? What else could have done this? Not that legend, which haunted the minds of some bewildered farmers in

Upstate Michigan, who really believed in that dogman myth. I mean really, why should such a thing as the dogman really exist, I thought to myself, not knowing, that I must have been very bold and arrogant at that moment.

But this is the way I thought then, what else should one expect from a rational biologist, a man of science, who denied or at least tried to avoid confrontation with paranormal phenomena, because of their, according to my knowledge of science then, unscientific elements, which made it really hard to grasp such phenomena and prove it scientifically. So I stepped into my car on this early morning on the 26 of February and was not even the slightest ready for what was about to happen.

But how should I have known, if I denied these things, which from my own experience are as real as our breath.

Perhaps it is this arrogance of most scientists, which actually stops them from encountering such things, perhaps the minds of concrete can only open up if they are confronted with things, which they cannot explain, but still, perceive or even sometimes measure scientifically. I started the motor of my car and everything went smooth for the next hour or so.

I drove past my lane, past the streets of Milwaukee, which would lead me to my first stop Appleton on my trip to my ranch. Everything would change though, or better formulated, started alternating, as my car was on the highway. I must have been driving for ten minutes or so on the highway, as I noticed a strange car, a little truck following me and keeping up my pace, but still keeping a distance of about fifty feet. I could see the drivers reflection in the windows of my car and his eyes, the expression of his face exuded gloominess and a sort of creepiness, that gave me a slight unease. This was the first thing, which was bizarre, but soon something else would happen, which also was very queer.

10 Minutes later, I could see a woman hitchhiking. She was holding a board which read: „Can you take me to ...". „What the heck, this is strange, why is this woman holding this board? Should I stop or not?" he thought to himself, pondering whether he should stop his car or not. After hesitating for a while, I decided to stop the car and take the woman, because she was heading into the same direction, she wanted to go to Burnett County, the place where I had my farm. The woman said: „O, thank you very much, Sir. I am so glad, that you are taking me for a lift." and hopped inside the car. I looked at her and smiled trying to be as kind and friendly as I could, in spite of the problems and

worries, which were pestering my mind and responded: „No, problem, I am going to Burnett County too, but I'll make some stops if you don't mind." The woman smiled and answered: „Ok, no problem, where are you going to stop?" I thought for a while and then I said very slowly and quietly: „Well actually I wanted to go to Appleton first for a coffee and then maybe Wausau and It still was quite a drive to the farm and I decided to make little detour to Appleton, where I wanted to have a cup of good fresh coffee. Hence I drove to Watertown and took the highway to Appleton from there. It started to rain and some clouds formed in the sky.

A query sense of something pervaded my atmosphere. The woman was silent and only started to say something after twenty minutes of driving or so. Then she said: „Thank you so much again for taking me, I never thought, that someone from Milwaukee was going to Burnett County. You must have some family there or something?" I glanced at here from my driver's seat and said: „No, actually I just own a farm there, but that is quite a long story. You seem to be very curious – aren't you?"

The woman looked at me and answered: „Well I am from there and just have finished my work in Milwaukee. Due to some financial problems, I could not find another to go there. I am from Burnett County by the way and we tend to be very open folk, I guess you know that." I went taciturn for a second and then I responded chuckling: „Yeah, You're right, you folks up there are different from us." Soon I could see Lake Winnebago to my right and it was quiet this time. Part of the lake seemed to be frozen and I was amazed by the tranquility, that it was purveying.

Then I just could not be quiet anymore, this placidity was choking me and I made up my mind to start a conversation with the woman sitting in my car. „Do you know, that this lake was special to the Indian tribe of the Menominee. Have you actually ever bathed in Fox river? It is not so cold during spring and summer, I must admit. This lake is by the way also called Kitchigamina Lake. I think it is the largest Lake of this state. Did you know that? Well, it doesn't really matter, I am just mentioning it because it always has some aura to me." I said while I was driving at about 50 miles an hour and almost had arrived at the middle of the lake.

A moment of silence passed and then the woman responded: „No I really was not aware of the Menominee living here, although I have heard of this tribe. And I also didn't know, that the lake Winnebago is also called

Kitchigamina and that it is the largest Lake of Wisconsin. I think it is fascinating, You seem to be very well informed. Most people don't read nowadays and I like it, when someone has something to tell, besides some sports event and a tv show or soap opera. But I too would like to share something with you, if I may. There actually is a good reason, why I am going to Burnett County and that is more than just seeing my folks again. Some people have told me, that some cattle have gone missing and some farmers claim to have seen a creature, which is rumored to haunt the forests of Burnett County. Have you ever heard of the dogman?" I shuddered, that could not be true, what she just had uttered.

Was she saying, that I was not the only one, who was affected? But this creature called *dogman*, could just not be real or could it? I shivered and almost lost the balance of my steering wheel. „Come one please, everyone knows, that the dogman is a mere myth, a figment of our imagination. There is no such thing as a dogman, don't you know that. I was a man of science can prove this, although science cannot prove everything and they're probably are still many unsolved mysteries out there, the dogman is just a made-up fantasy of some deranged lunatics. This my opinion, but I know, that you want to see this otherwise, which is perfectly fine with me, but I will not see it, the way some folk see it, until I have seen and examined such a creature myself, although I know, that this won't happen, because the dogman simply does not exist. Do you understand." I told her with a coarse tone.

She just glanced at me and said: „Well, if that is so, then why have some many people seen him. This creature has been seen for centuries and You just cannot believe it, because your science tells you that right? Well then please tell me why there are so many phenomena out there, which it can't explain." Now I was angry, but I restrained myself from arguing, why should I, I knew, that I was right. But now I know, that I was so bold and arrogant and conditioned by some mainstream brainwashed science, that was clueless, when it came to such phenomena. I must say, that I still can comprehend a scientist, who denies the dogman because it is simply out of this world and will cause you to fear the woods and rethink your view of the world. I guess, that many scientists don't have the guts to rethink their world view and that is why they just jeer when they hear of these constant reports. Or maybe they are just not informed enough to realize, that these things really exist.

Time flew by and soon we had arrived in Appleton, where I found a nice coffeehouse, which I called by more than once in my life. As we entered it, I could sense something strange, which I cannot put into words. Perhaps I know now, what it was, maybe some sort of precognitive sentiment, which foretold me something, that I could only understand after having this amazing experience with the dog man, which actually almost cost me my life.

We sat down on a table and ordered some coffee. The woman stared at me and thanked me for the coffee, which she drank with one gulp. We had a short conversation about some unimportant issues, which I now would not like to address because they did not touch the matter of this story, which is my personal encounter with the alleged dog man, who I denied until I had the personal experience.

After an hour or so we left the coffeehouse and drove to Wausau, which was another drive of at least two hours or so. As we were driving through the town of Wausau the feeling, which I had whilst entering the coffeehouse returned for some time. Something was queer and I did not really know why. I started thinking, that something or someone was following o rat least watching us.

The stop in Wausau was quite brief and the feeling became stronger, which gave me a great sense of unease. Then we left Wausau and drove to Grantsburg, which was a three-hour drive. I asked the woman, I fit would be fine with here, if I didn't make another stop, because I wanted to be at my ranch before six p.m.. She just said, „Yes, okay with me." The drive to Grantsburg was very calm and quiet and soon darkness spread across the land of Wisconsin.

As I arrived in Grantsburg, I decided to drop the woman off there and asked her: „Is it okay with you, if I leave you here, or should I drive you directly to your family's address?" Silenced surrounded us and then she spoke with an eery expression on her face, which kind of gave me the creeps: „No, this is fine with me, I will contact my family, no problem. Just let me out here ok." So I let her out at the next crossing and headed towards my ranch, which was only a few miles away from Grantsburg.

After about 15 minutes of driving, I arrived at the gates of my ranch and a cold wind greeted me, as I stepped outside my car. I opened the gate and closed it again. The private road to my house was an about three to four miles long and there the weirdest things happened, which I am about to explain because they would be the first omen of my encounter with a beast, that would challenge even the most stable person.

At the beginning of my private road about two hundred yards away from the gate, I saw a shadow of something in the back mirror of my car. It was the shadow of something big and I had problems deciphering what it could actually be because I was only able to see the outlines of its shadow which had a greyish touch to it. Then after a short while, I saw it again, or at least a very similar shadow of that sort, but this time it came from the other side of the road, moving extremely fast. I was amazed because I had never seen such a shadow. This time though I was capable of perceiving more details of the shadow.

The shadow had a dog like a figure or some sort of wolf. Suddenly the conversations with the woman, whom I had picked up, popped up in my mind. Was she right, were there really obscure things going on in this part of Wisconsin, which had t be labeled unexplainable? What was I thinking, this could not be real and then just after I had molded this notion my care bumped into something, which was big. I stopped the car for a sec, but when I looked out the window, I only could something running past my car and running into the darkness on the side of the road. The darkness was there, because I had never thought of constructing lampposts on the side of the road, so the road was not lit, and this of course was a disadvantage, especially on cold winter nights such as this one. I started the car again and recommenced my driving, but just after another while or so, I could hear a loud howl, which must have been coming from nearby.

Naive and stable as I still was at this point of my story, I ignored it and concentrated on my driving. But after another moment or so I heard it again, although this time it was long and seemed to be more intense. Then after a minute or so yet again I heard another howl, which was followed by some snarling growls. „What kind of dog is this, I can't remember hearing or seeing any dog, that does this kind of stuff?" I thought whilst continuing my driving. Now, this was starting to become weirder and weirder and I must admit, that I was already quite spooked out, in spite of trying to keep calm and stable.

Then it happened, something, which I could not have imagined in my wildest dreams. Just about a mile away from my ranch, after a sharp turn on the right, next to a hill and a small forest, which I could see from my ranch, I saw a figure, which was maybe about 50 yards ahead of me, standing on it's hind legs in the middle of my private road. The figure was that of a dog and I looked at it many times because I could not believe my eyes. This figure was hairy and the lights of my car enabled me to see the details of its makeup. The figure's reddish eyes were staring at me and I decided to pull the brakes and turn off the motor of my car. I locked myself inside the car, just to make sure and looked at this figure in uttermost awe. Then the figure walked towards me and stopped about 10 yards in front of my car. Now I had no doubt in my mind, that what was standing in front of me could only be a dogman.

A dogman, but a dogman was just some fictitious superstitious story of some Indian tribes, this could not be real or could it? The dogman or whatever it was to me at that moment growled and snarled at me and its eyes had something evil to it, which I cannot put into words. This beast had a canine face and a large snout with big teeth, which hung like fangs out of its mouth. Shear horror now was spreading into the deepest core of my soul and mind. This was the real Mccoy, this was a dogman, and it was wanting something from me. But what could it want? Should I be its next supper? Was it playing with me? Was it perhaps feeding of my fear? I was not sure, but what I was sure of is, that I had to do something, because just sitting there, would just aggravate my situation.

So I started my car again and tried to dodge the creature, whilst driving. As I passed it, the dogman just stood there and I was really close to it now and that scared the hell out of me. Now I could really see how massive this beast was. Its shoulders were very wide and it's height must have been at least 10 feet or probably more. My heart started pounding and I drove at a slow speed now, hoping not to provoke this beast. „What would I do though, when I arrived at my ranch? Should I call the cops or should I just lock my doors and barricade all the windows, grab my guns and wait till the morning? What about my workers, could they perhaps help me? Should I call them?" I thought totally desperate and confused.

I knew very well, that the cops would not believe me and the workers, could not help me now because they were already at their homesteads, which were at least 20 to thirty miles from my ranch. The only thing, that I could do was to drive to the ranch and talk to my two servants, who stayed there full time. So I drove to my ranch and tried to mitigate my worried soul.

As I arrived at the ranch, the lights were luckily lit, so I got out of my car and rang the doorbell. One of my servants called Bill opened the door and said: „Glad you made it, is everything alright with you? You look a little distressed?" I looked at the bill and sighed: „Oh, yes I am very happy, that I have made it. I hope, that you have the guns loaded, there is something out there and it is massive and very ferocious." After saying that I entered the door, which bill locked behind me. „Yes sir we have some guns loaded and actually we wanted to tell you about this beast, but I guess, that you know now. It is hard to believe something like this exists until you meet it eye to eye. I guess you are a believer now, aren't you? I'll get you some coffee and I'll call some workers and tell them, that they should bring some rifles. Your dam was lucky if you've seen to believe it. This dogman ain't a puppy." Bill chuckled and got me some coffee.

I decided to go into my saloon and read some book, to forget what had just happened. But how could I expulse this horrible event, which just had occurred me, if it had marked me for life? The next hours which followed this ghastly experience would, as I later found out, be the worst of my life because this would not be the end of this horror, it was just the beginning. The old clock in my saloon was ticking as always and I began to take sips of the coffee, which kind old Bill had brought me. Bill was a good man of 60 years of age and he had been a very loyal servant to me and my family. Bill was part Indian and he was very well acquainted with the dogman, for it had haunted the minds of his tribe for centuries.

Just as I was sitting on my favorite sofa, reading a book on rural economics, I could hear steps, loud thumps outside the ranch. Then the shadow of a doglike figure shone through the window, which was about 30 feet away from me. „What was going on, this can't be real. Why did this beast roam around my ranch and what was its goal?" I thought, shuddering with fear and keeping quiet. Bill was standing outside of the saloon and holding a rifle and there was the other servant Pete, who also had a gun in his hand and revolver in his holster.

The tension grew and the silence was our companion, but not for very long. „So Bill have you contacted the workers yet? Are they coming?" I asked still perplex and in a total haze. „Most didn't respond to my call, but two are on their way. They're bringing some friends with them, but they told me, that they will take a few hours, because of some blizzard and some time, that they need to organize some more guns, I hope you can understand. " he answered very calmly without any fear. „Of course I can, I am glad, that they can come anyway. Thank you for calling them!" I responded and read another page of my book on rural economics.

The minutes passed and then we all could hear vicious howls around the ranch. The dogman was close by, that was all, that I knew. It must have been near the barn because the last howl was coming from that direction. The barn near my main house of the ranch, which was just 150 feet away. Then it started to snow and wind accompanied the snow whistling ominous tokens of unprecedented doom. „Would this be my last day? The last day of my life? If so, then then I would like to die in peace and not in pain." I thought, still reading the book about rural economics.

Then I heard another howl, followed by some scratching, which seemed to come from the front door. „Was the dogman so close? Was it trying to intimidate me and my servants? Was it a game, which is played before it preyed on its victims?" I wondered, trying to cope with my anxiety and my fear, which was quite tremendous now. „Bill is there an antidote to this? Does the dogman fear something? Is yes please let me know? Every creature must have some kind of weakness?" I asked him with a loud voice, which to some extent was a mistake, because then the howling and scratching noises returned, but this time more intense than before.

After a while they stopped and then Bill, who was thinking, answered my question: „Yes the dogman has weaknesses, one is a special herb, that gives of ascent, which it hates. Then I have heard, that it does not like a very bright light.

Stories of my tribe seem to confirm this." "Thank you Bill, so where can we get that herb or how can we create a light, that scares it off?" I inquired further.

Bill responded with a very resonated tone in his voice: "Well the herb should grow on your ranch and the light could be creating a big bonfire. A burning torch should do the job as well, I guess." "Good, so where can I get such a torch, is there one in the barn? This herb what is it called or how does it look like?"

I asked on, getting more anxious by the minute. Bill looked at me and said: "There should be a torch in the barn, but I would not go out now if I were you. The dogman will sense you and probably tear you to pieces. Looking for the herb, which is also senseless at this time of year and especially at night. The herb is called clematis Aristolochia or just commonly known as birthwort." I stared at Bill again and told him: „Thank you for the information! What should we do instead? Are there still any other options or not?" A moment of silence passed between me and Bill and then a few howls penetrated the night, which seemed to be further away. „Well, I guess that we can defeat it with our firepower, so the best thing, that we can do ist to stay in the house. I can sense, that it has distanced itself from the ranch, but it probably could come back still, so we should wait until morning."

Bill responded with a quiet tone to his voice. I glanced at him and at my other servant Pete and then I said: „Okay, let's just wait. Could you please make a fire, because I am of the opinion, that it is quite chilly." Andrew and Bill gazed at me for a second and said: „Of course Sir, we will heat the house, but it might take a while until the house is really warm. If something strange should happen in the meanwhile please feel free to call us, you can ring us on our cell phones." „Thank you, Bill and Pete, I'll stay here and finish reading my book. Please inform, when the workers arrive. Tell them to come inside and guard the upper floors of the house, this is going to be a long night. Till later." I said with a kind tone.

So I continued reading my book and time passed. The clocked ticked and soon an hour or more had passed. It was quiet now, just the whistling wind outside was audible. After a while I guess, I must have fallen into a short slumber because the sound of cars woke me up. The front door opened and men entered the house. „Sir, the workers have arrived and the house is well heated now. Pete and I are staying downstairs with you if this is okay for you sir? Please instruct the workers and talk to them." Bill told me, standing right next to me not far from the door, which led to my saloon, as I was just in the process of waking up and realizing, that I had slept for at least three hours. „Yeah sure, let the gentleman in the saloon. I'll instruct them and thank you for heating the house, I can feel, that it is definitely warmer than a few hours ago."

Bill went to the door and opened it and after a very short while eight men entered the saloon. The men were holding guns in their hands and two of them were my workers Jim and Chuck. „Please take a sit fellow, I have a matter to discuss. There is a dogman running around my ranch and I am sorry for my disbelief. Now I am a believer and I would ask you to guard the upper floors. This beast has been walking around the house and it is very aggressive, so show no mercy if it tries to break into the house. Jim, go with Chuck now and check out the first floor and tell your six friends, that they should guard the second floor and the attic. This is all very new to me and I don't know how to react in such a situation." „Ok, the boss we will do that. Should we call you if something happens?" Jim asked me? I thought for an instant and then responded with a calm and slightly disturbed voice: „Yes, please call me on my cell phone or send me an SMS." But do not hesitate to shoot." „Okay Boss, we will do that." Jim said and left the saloon with Chuck and their eight friends.

The door closed behind them and now I was alone again in my big saloon on accompanied by my old clock, which was ticking like some timeless object from another dimension. Minutes passed and then hours, and I was starting to calm down again when suddenly I heard some strange growling and shots being fired afterward. I looked at the clock and it was way past midnight, it was 3 a. m.

„What was going on? Should I grab my gun and check out, what had just taken place? Or should I stay here and wait?" I thought not really knowing what had actually happened. Then the door opened and Bill and Pete ran inside the saloon.

They were out of breath and seemed to be very distressed. „What is wrong? Can you please tell me what has just occurred?" „Well sir, two of the worker's friend are missing, one his dead and the others are on the first floor and have fired multiple shots at the dogman, which broke into a window and killed on of their friends. Jim and Chuck are okay though, but they are quite scared. The dogman has managed to lure two of their friends outside, by imitating some familiar voice, I know, this sounds very eerie and I just am saying, what they told me. This, by the way, happened an hour before it tried to get into the house." Pete said trembling with fear. „Okay, but I told them, that they should inform me if something weird was going on. Tell them to lock all the doors on the first floor and join me in the saloon." I responded nervously. „Okay, sir." Pete and Bill said instantaneously.

Pete and Bill headed upstairs and I heard them talking to Jim and Chuck and the other workers. Soon after that, I could hear them hurrying down the stairs and the door to my saloon opened. Jim and Chuck were pale as the snow outside of the house and the other workers had a very sullen look on their face. „Please sit down and tell me, what happened." I said in a calm voice.

Jim and Chuck sat down on the chairs next to my favorite couch and the others took a seat at the table, which was approximately 15 feet behind my couch. „First we heard voices and two of our friends decided to check them out. These voices seemed to have to lead them on the balcony and since then, we have not heard from them. We checked the balcony on the second floor twice and there is no trace of blood or a body part, nothing. Then about an hour later we could hear growls and then this greyish looking dogman broke into one window and attacked one of us. It was Mark, it ripped him to shreds, it was horrible, so horrible. We fired at it with all our firepower, which made it leap out of the window and flee. I think, that it is at least injured, but I've heard stories, that these creatures can heal their wounds very quickly. We then took Marks body into the cellar, where we put him in a chest. After that, we informed the police and told them, that one of our friends has had a fatal accident. The police told us, that they would send someone to the ranch, but did not know how long it would take, because of the blizzard." Chuck told me with fear in his eyes. „What the hell, Mark one of your friends is dead and that dogman is still on the loose and the cops aren't coming soon, what the... I don't understand this county, but I guess we have to fend it off if it comes again. Damn this is really a nightmare. Do we have enough ammo, or are you already out of it?" I responded by being very tense and worried. „We still have some rounds, but there must be some more in the barn. We usually store a lot of it in there. So I guess we have to go to the barn and get some. There should be a pump gun and a machine gun there too. Some friend of a worker left it there one day." Jim said totally scared and frightened. „Well then, if this is our only chance, I'll go to the barn with you guys and your friends, Bill and Pete stay in the saloon and lock all the doors to the saloon. I'll knock three times, to let them know, that it is us, meaning you Jim and me." I explained.

Chuck looked at me and said: „Okay, let's go, I'll grab two flashlight sand give you cover with Jim." A moment passed and I was not really realizing, what I had just uttered, but what other option was there really? Waiting with fewer rounds and no machine gun, or waiting with more rounds and a machine gun. „Let's go. Get Bill and Pete and wait in the saloon and lock all the doors to the saloon." I said to the five friends of Chuck and Jim, whilst grabbing my gun and loading it. I stood up and left the saloon with Chuck and Jim, and my world was totally out of balance.

This could not be real, this horror, which I honestly still cannot comprehend. As I opened the front door of the house a cold wind greeted me with some insidious omen, which gave me chills in my spine. Slowly I made my way to the barn with Chuck and Jim behind me, pointing their guns at everything in front of me. Their flashlights were lighting my way. Soon I reached the barn after walking through the fresh snow and the cold wind, which seemed to create a very creepy atmosphere.

As I reached the barn door, I searched for the proper key and took a while to find it. The moment I opened the door to the barn, something dashed passed me, Jim and Chuck. It was big and grey, that is all that I could see and then it happened. A growling sound entailing a loud howl filled the cold air and I turned to see what was going on.

I stood in total awe. Standing about 60 feet away from Jim and Chuck were the dogman. And now I really could estimate it's height. It was at least 10 feet tall and a had massive shoulders and a very canine face. The eyes seemed to be of a reddish hue. Jim and Chuck turned and as they turned the dogman charged. They fired and kept on firing until the dogman grazed Chuck with one of its claws before jumping away in pain because I could see, that they had hit it badly. We hurried into the barn quickly and closed the door behind us.

After that, I started searching for the machine gun and the pump gun and asked Jim, who was standing right next to me and shedding light on the barn: „Do you have any idea where the machine gun and the pump gun could be?" Jim answered briskly: „Yeah I'll show you were they should be." and lead me past the stacks of tools and piles of wood to the end of the barn, while Chuck was guarding the door and staring out the window next to the barn's door watching every move in the dark and snowy landscape.

Just when we arrived at the end of the barn, Jim pointed at the right side of the barn, where I could see two bags and next to them a shotgun and a machinegun. „Great, the guns are there, but are they loaded and are there any bullets for them here or in the house?" I asked with some relief. „Pete and Bill must have some ammo for them in the house, but I guess, that the guns are neither loaded nor that there is any ammo for them here. We have to head back now and avid the dogman at any cost. Perhaps I can distract it by lighting some firecrackers, which could distract it. If I light them, we must run quickly to the house and get inside fast. The dogman can move extremely fast and I don't want to end like Mark if you don't mind." Jim said with uncertainty in his being. „Okay, let's do that." I uttered.

We headed back to the entrance of the barn, me carrying the pump gun and Jim carrying the machine gun, where Chuck was waiting for us and then suddenly the dogman appeared right outside the barn's window. It growled and then broke the window. Chuck jumped aside and fired a couple of shots. The beast lashed out through the broken window but jolted back as I pulled the trigger of my pistol, which I had tucked inside my jacket. „Quickly, quickly, run to the house, I'll light the crackers now." Jim muttered. „Okay." I answered and ran to the house with Chuck and then swiftly opened the door with my key, which I had put in the left pocket of my trousers.

Just as the crackers were lit, Jim hurried towards us, as we already were inside, holding our guns and waiting. Just as he made it inside, the dogman appeared and charged at us again. We slammed the door shut and locked it. The dogman thumped against the door and scratched it with its claws. We ran to the saloon and I knocked three times, whilst the dogman was still thumping and scratching.

What a horror this was and I was scared, that it would manage to pry open the door and devour us. The door to the salon opened and we went inside, closing the door behind us. The scratching and thumping stopped, but then the dogman appeared in front of the windows of the saloon and smashed the windows. I, Pete, Bill, Jim, Chuck, and their remaining friends fired.

As my pistol was out of ammo, I tossed the machine gun at Pete and the pump gun at Bill, who caught it in mid-air and fired two rounds, which hit the snout of the dogman. The dogman, who seemed to be immune to most of the bullets, screamed ou loud and was thrust backward, probably by the bullets of the pump gun.

And then it finally fled and disappeared from my property forever, because from that day on it was never seen again. The nightmare was over, but what would I tell Mark's family and what had happened to the two workers, who had gone missing ever since that day, which has changed my whole life. But now I know of this beast and I thank god, that he spared my life that day and that most of us survived this terrible experience, which one can only understand if one has had such a similar experience because it is too macabre to ghastly to really describe. So this is my story avid reader. Make of it what you will.

The End

The Dogman of British Columbia

In the forests of British Columbia lies a dreaded secret, which is about to be unwrapped. There are many lakes and beautiful forests in the land of the most western frontier. But most are not aware, what really lies hidden in the beautiful mountains and forests of British Columbia. So, think twice while you roam around the seemingly peaceful land, which not only contains the sasquatch but other things as well, which are so dreadful, that most will never accept this to be true. Hence join me, Peter Cane, now, as I try to explain to you and paint you the events of my encounters with one of the most cryptic creatures, which are as real as you and I.

The story of my first experience with a Dogman begins, when I was small and very young. I cannot exactly recall, how old I was, but I know, that I must have been around four or five, when I had my first encounter with a creature, which is known under many names, most commonly under the name "Dogman". At that time, when I was young, I used to play near my parent's house, in an old shed, which belonged to an old farmer, who lived about a mile away from us. We were living near the Rocky Mountains and there were many farms in our vicinity. I really loved the pastures and soft fields, especially in summer, they were really amazing. But one day, I think it must have been fall, I am not sure, but I can remember, that the leaves already had the touch of autumn in their essence and most trees had red, yellow and brown leaves, which in all gave them a wonderful spectrum of many shades of various colors.

On this day I was playing with a friend of mine, or should I say a friend of my childhood. We were sitting in the grass not far from the old barn, as we suddenly saw something move in the nearby forest. It was a fury looking creature and it reminded me of a bear, but it was walking upright, which made me wonder because bears normally did not walk upright. The creature had a slender build and was somewhat canine in appearance. I don't know exactly how tall it was, but I am sure, that it must have been at least 8 foot or more. We stared at it in amazement, and because of this we were neither taken by surprise nor seemingly scared.

Maybe it was also the daylight, which gave us strength, because at night these things, are truly a lot scarier, than during daytime. This may have something to do with the creature itself. According to many legends, creatures of such manner, usually don't like to wander during the day, because they fear the light because it represents the creator of our infinite reality. Perhaps that could make sense, but let me carry on with my story, my further accounts of meeting or having contact with this creature and another, which could be classified as some sort of hybrid. After we had noticed the creature walking, it finally stopped and just stared at us and snarled for a moment and then vanished and when I say "vanished" I mean it. The creature just vanished from one moment to the next. And that, if I reminisce about that moment correctly, really gave me the creeps. How could such an animal, such a thing, just simply vanish, without a trace. I and my friend searched the area around the barn and there were really now traces, no footprints of this creature. So, this was my first encounter with the Dogman, let me share another one with you, which was a bit more vivid and real, than the first one. I think I must have been nine or ten, I am not sure, but I think, that it really doesn't matter. I was hiking with an Uncle in the Rockies, not very far from my parent's house. I guess it would have been about 30 miles or so.

Well, distance is a bit different to us, so bear in mind, that the term "close" is always relative, but let's say, that I was not more than an hour's drive away from my parent's house and I was enjoying the mountains. My Uncle owned an old cabin, which was a log cabin, stemming from the nineteenth century and he used to go to it with me multiple times. This time though, I think it must have been not very far from the cabin, about a mile I would say, looking back and trying to figure out, which memory occurred first. I could hear something following me. At first, I just ignored it, but then I thought to myself, that it was strange, because the sounds I heard, reminded me of the creature, whom I had encountered when I was little. The more I thought about this circumstance, the more my mind was trembling by the very thought of having to realize, that I was in the proximity of another creature, which is known under the name "Dogman". I remember, that I could not talk for the rest of our hike to the cabin. as we arrived I muttered: "Uncle, I think, that I have seen a Dogman and I believe, that there might be a given chance, that it is following us." My uncle looked at me, slightly squinting his eyes and then spoke with his usual harsh but not bad spoken British Columbian slang: "Hey son, calm down, the Dogman is not real, there are just wolves and bears out there. Although some folks believe, that there is the slim possibility of some Sasquatch roaming these forests, they are mostly harmless: so don't worry son!" I was absolutely in shock for a moment and thought, that I was in the wrong film. My uncle just had acknowledged, that something as a Sasquatch is real, but a Dogman is not. What kind of an oxymoron is that, when someone approves of one thing but denies the other. Well, sadly my uncle was one of these types, in spite of always meaning well, because he was one of the last pioneers, albeit one of the last people, who really inhaled the freedom of the wilderness, but at the same time showed great respects for the Indian tribes of the area, who he tended to call the real Canadian — a term which might sound very controversial and disgusting to some three- or even five generational Canadian, who of course will see himself as a real Canadian, but probably had not even once in his whole life smelled the fresh grass of the Rocky Mountains or gazed at the lush green and amber hue of the cedars, pines or sequoia trees of the Pacific coast. This is simply, because these Canadians, were, what my uncle considered to be so-called "cozy Canadians". I know, that this sounds like a strange term and maybe it is, who am I to judge — but honestly, I could not be amazed, because my uncle was a real exception, maybe even a very alienated species of some forgotten time, but still my uncle.

I and my uncle went into the cabin and he, a real hoser, got some log, which was stacked not very far away from the cabin. My mood seemed to quieten down a bit and everything was getting better, at least for a moment. I don't recall, when the beast, the Dogman appeared again, because I had a very odd and eerie feeling, that I was being watched by someone, rather by something I can say from my today's point of view. A mixture of fear and solitude caressed my still slightly distorted mental state and I was trying to think of something else but the Dogman, although I knew, that it was always present in my mind. The time passed quickly and every minute was an eternity to me, for I was deeply indulging, albeit unwillingly, driven by my fears and anxieties, which I was not able to control, into my world of thoughts. "Hi yu, would you like some kokanee you skookum kid?" my uncle's voice penetrated through the cabin and woke me up out of my state of distraught numbness and worries, which had truly encompassed me whilst he had gone out to fetch some wood. "No, thanks! I'll just eat some marshmallow if you have some? Can we make a fire, when it gets dark?" I said, hoping to finally relax and enjoy the beautiful wilderness of the Rocky Mountains. "Ye okay, I'll just get the oven starting in the cabin and then we can make a little campfire nearby. Hope you have recovered from your experiences kid. Don't worry it was just some odd animal, you know, some of them just turn out to be a bit bigger and a weeny bit different than the rest." my uncle muttered.

I looked him in the eye and said:" Uncle. I guess, that everything is okay, but still, some fears are lingering inside me. Hope, that you got the fire already going?" My uncle seemed to be in a short kind of haze and then responded: "Yes, I have, but the fire needs some to burn well. But don't worry kid, it will be really scorching in just a sec." So, I waited and time went past, but not for my individual sense of time. Everything seemed to be very awkward and odd, and I had that feeling again, that same sentiment, which I had when I saw that Dogman, whilst walking on the trail to the cabin. I was sure, that it must have been lurking somewhere, watching us and maybe wanting to attack us, who could have known that for sure.

Then my uncle popped up again and said with a slightly disgruntled voice:" Come on boy, let's roast some marshmallows! I guess that the fire is okay now, although it doesn't seem to burn, the way it should. Yikes, I guess, that is the way things go sometimes. Grab the bag of marshmallows and chuck it over to me. Oh, before I forget, you can dry your gotch, if you want to. You know, that the pond is not very far away and a swim would do you good!" "Okay uncle, I'll fetch the bag and join you in no time!" I muttered with a quiet and tainted voice, for the fears had already taken control over me and I did not know, how I could successfully restrain them, albeit get rid of them. Somehow I managed to recover and regain some of my courage. I joined my uncle, who already was sitting next to the fire and roasting some marshmallows. I took a seat next to him and tried to forget everything, that I had experienced, although I was totally aware, that that would be a very arduous task for me to fulfill. It did not take long until the daylight faded away and the darkness of the night crept upon us like a lurking shadow of some unknown place in time. For a while, everything seemed fine, but then I sensed, that something was moving in the forest behind us. Something, which was exuding terror and malignity, which I could not really describe, for it was too hard to grasp, especially for a young boy of 11 years. Then a terrible howl penetrated our silent company. The howl was vicious and it was followed by snarling and various growls and more silent howls, which according to me were even worse because they contained more uncanniness than the first one. My uncle became nervous and his face turned more and more anxious. This was the moment, that he started believing the things, which I had been telling him since my encounter on the trail with this thing, which many call "Dogman". "Ok, the kid we got a situation going on here. This is not a wolf and not a sasquatch. I have to admit, that it is kinda freaking me out and that we maybe should return to the cabin and lock it from inside. Are you ready? We go in one, two, three seconds, okay?" he whispered. I just nodded, but before my uncle could utter another word, the Dogman, who had been encircling us, leaped out of the forest, grabbed my uncle by his shoulders and dragged him into the forest. This happened so fast, that I was in total shock for a moment. The only thing, that I had heard from my uncle, were his screams, which vanished in the forest. I was shaking and extremely scared, but I tried to keep my cool and hurried into the cabin, locking it from the inside. My heart was pounding now and I did not know, what was going to happen next, so I started praying to soothe my mixed emotions of agony, despair, and fear. After a while, I could hear some sounds coming from the forest. Branches and twigs were cracking and then I saw the shadow of the Dogman towering over the cabin. The Dogman could not have been more than 20 feet away from it now and its red eyes were staring at something, but not at me. In total shock and fear, I was cowering on the floor of the cabin.

The steps of the Dogman were heading towards the cabin and I could feel its encroaching evil presence. It did not take long until I could hear it scratch against the wooden walls of the cabin, whilst snorting and snarling in the most vicious manner, which I could ever envisage. I don't know how long it took, until this beast, this monster left, for I was utterly petrified by its presence and actually did not know, whether I would survive to tell the tale. As you see I could, and I am so glad, that god, that fate had spared my life.

So, this is the story of my most vivid encounters with the Dogman, which I had and will most certainly always remember. I reckon, that they were the most interesting ones and I guess, that the other ones, would be, to be correct, mere sightings of this beast and were only lasted for a very short time. Sadly my uncles death was one of the dire aftermaths associated with this cryptid, this monster, although I don't want to be judgmental and bear a grudge against every Dogman, because who am I, who would have the right to judge every one of these creatures, who may be just as good and bad as we are. Hence be vigilant if you should wander in the wilderness of British Columbia because you never know whom you should encounter and the Dogman is just one of many creatures of myth, who dwell in the vast mountains and wonderful forest of British Columbia.

The End

The Dogman of Germany

What a strange thing, to fathom, that such a creature could exist in a place like Germany, where reason and nowadays decadence prevails, but that is all in all another question, which I will not expound on for now. But not only the Dogman roams the forests of the once so great country of the poets and thinkers, no: there are supposedly many other cryptids dwelling in Germany's last resorts of nature, which once sprawled across the whole lands of the German culture, which more and more is waning, to maybe embrace its grave.

So, deep in the Taunus mountains at the beginning of the 21st century, a brave woman, who loved nature, had the decision to move into the mountains and live there in a little house with a very adorable patio. The woman, who was a brave shaman and a good mother, fell in love with the beautiful surroundings of the Taunus mountain range, which still resembled some of the old glory of Germanic lore, which now has been long forgotten; probably because of the very sad and somber past, which still haunts most Germans and German-speaking people.

One day the shaman woman, who was called Amaroca, was walking late at night on the path leading to her house. She was wondering as always, but suddenly she could hear movement in the nearby trees. She stopped and began to tremble with fear as she could see the image of a huge black thing causing the earth around her to shake. For a moment she could not even breath while this thing passed her, not even taking the slightest interest in her, and disappearing again into the mystic depth of the forest.

Then after a while as the thumping thundering steps of this beast of unknown nature, disappeared into the belly of the night, she hurried back home, where she was not able to pacify her mind, at least for the rest of the night.

But this was not her only encounter, which she would have with this creature, whom she later would recognize as a Dogman. But how could she have known, that what she just had witnessed was a Dogman, if most people in Germany did not even know that the word "Dogman" exists let alone had been roaming the forests of Germany for centuries.

The days passed and Amaroca calmed down and began to reorganize her emotional state and her life. But the encounter, that she had had still was haunting her mind and she did not know, how she could really deal with this.

But because of her character, she opted to not let herself be intimidated by this beast and began to walk and wander again through the forest at night, which she really savored, because of the trees and their individual fragrance.

So, after a week or more had passed, she was once again walking in the forest, but did not wander too far into the forest. As she stared at the crescent moon and picked up some rare mushrooms, she could suddenly see a tall figure, standing about 200 yards in front of her and smelling something, which she was not able to perceive from, where she was.

The figure seemed to be very indulged in that, what it was doing, but then it turned its canine head and stared at here with its menacing eyes. Amaroca was petrified, and just could not move, paralyzed by the shock and angst, which was caused by the ferocious eyes of this doglike creature.

Slowly this doglike creature came towards her and stopped about 50 feet away from her. Amaroca just stood very still and did not move even a tenth of an inch. For a moment the creature just stood there and observed here and then it passed her again, as one of her first encounters, although this time Amaroca was just standing 15 feet away, as this doglike creature passed her, who as she later found out was a Dogman and probably was one of her first encounters, although she still doubts this thesis at times.

Five minutes after the Dogman had passed her, walking bipedal and smelling everything around it, she slowly returned to the path, which leads to her small but cozy house. There she started her research on cryptids and found out, that there were many stories concerning these doglike creatures.

And then she drew the conclusion, that what she had seen probably was a Dogman, a creature, that was not supposed to exist, and this notion of perceiving, experiencing something, which should not exist, made her headache and caused her many doubts of torment and nightmares, where she was being followed and chased by a Dogman.

Hence Amaroca started to be more vigilant, despite her braveness.

But something, some urge inside her, caused her to find out more about this creature, whom she wanted to get to know better, although she knew, that this curious yearning for more experiences with this ferocious beast, could cost her, her life.

The days went by and Amaroca spent more and more time with the research on the Dogman and other cryptids, who were supposed to roam the forests of Germany, at least the ones, which she was surrounded by. Deeper and Deeper she delved into the world of the cryptids and the dreams of the Dogman were not to cease, albeit change slightly in every dream.

So, it was no great surprise, that she would again encounter such another beast once again, as she was bravely wandering in the forest near her house, which was a safe haven, until now. It was another beautiful and magnificent day and the sun was shining at full strength as she would once again meet a Dogman, who probably had been observing her for quite a while.

The Dogman had brown fur and yellow eyes, which glared at her, penetrating her soul with the energy of an unseen force, which was emanating from it. Amaroca confronted the Dogman and said, whilst the Dogman was standing only 20 feet away from her: "What do you want? What is your purpose of following me?" For a second the Dogman did not respond, but then it growled and responded in a strange tone, trying to imitate the sound of a male human: "My dear, don't you know, that you are a chosen one? You are one of the few, who have the privilege of seeing us, for we don't appear to everyone. This is why we have been pursuing you for some time. Have you never thought why you have constant dreams about us? Has it not come to your mind, that we communicate, albeit are able to communicate via dreams."

"But, why am I chosen?" Amaroca answered swiftly, without even reflecting the words, coming out of her mouth. "You are chosen, because of your blood and the ancestry which entails it. You have Indian blood and your ancestors have always befriended our kind, don't you know that? Have you not realized, that there is a purpose to everything in life. Most men fear us, and they have a right to do so, but not all of our kind are evil; just like to every human is evil. The truth is always a grey shade and not black or white. Look at the trees, can't you see, that they have chosen to be trees? Listen to the birds, chirping, don't you comprehend, that they have made the choice to be birds? Don't you know the ways of your people, woman? And now open your eyes to nature and feel the breathing life, which is everywhere and all stems from one source, the source of eternal light, which emanates from Manitu or the Great Spirit, as the Indians call it. Cant you see, that everything is a part of everything and an expression from a divine and eternal God?" the Dogman explained in a harsh voice.

Amaroca sighed and glanced at the ferocious-looking Dogman, who was very quiet and calm, although his appearance was terrible and massive. "Okay, I think, that I have understood, what you have tried to convey with your words, but what is my purpose then, if I am a chosen one, as you say," Amaroca replied. "Well, this is the riddle, the conundrum, which you will have to solve. I may be of some assistance, but I will not help you solve your tasks, for it is written, that he, who seeks shall find. Don't you know that? Furthermore, you must understand, that the source, God, wants, that everyone should take on some responsibility and be self-sufficient in the ambiguous sense of the word, Amaroca. Interesting name by the way, for I really like the Indian names. I guess, that you really are yearning to be a wolf or should I say she-wolf.

But let me tell you and show you a bit more, so that you may finally grasp the ways of nature and its laws, which are still very new to you if I durst say that."

the Dogman answered in great detail.

Then the dogman gave her a wink to follow him deeper into the forest.

Amaroca was petrified at first, for she did not want to wander off so far from her house, but something, some form of intuition foretold her, that the Dogman did not mean her any harm; hence she followed the Dogman into the forest, trying to keep up with his fast stride.

After venturing into the forest for a half an hour, the Dogman led her to a well, which was in the middle of a pasture encircled by the forest. The Dogman stopped in front of the well and told her with a gentle, but the still profound tone in his voice: "Here it is. A symbol for the hunger and thirst of the Indian, who always tries to go inside his inner world to find his inner strength, from where the light from above should linger and radiate. Are you ready for your first task, which shall be a descent into this well, where you will be confronted with your most innate and strongest fear? Are you ready or shall we come again at a more convenient time, when are more mature?" Amaroca was stunned for a moment and tried to hide her anxieties and fears of descending into this well, which to her resembled some sort of hellish pit, some abyss, which she did not want to enter. Struggling with her fears, she gulped and replied: "Yes, I am prepared to go down. What shall I do then, shall I stay there?" The Dogman stared at here and said: "Yes, you shall stay there for a day and I will return and bring you back." "Okay," Amaroca responded, slightly shivering and trepidation with angst and fear of what could await here at the bottom of the well.

The Dogman took a rope, which was lying next to the well and tied it onto her and then he gently let her climb down the well, whilst holding the rope. Amaroca descended deeper and deeper into the well, which was dark and damp until she, at last, reached its bottom, which was at least 200 feet below the pasture.

She looked up to the Dogman, who appeared much smaller to her, than before and said: "I will untie the rope now and you can pull it up. I will wait here and see if I am able to survive this task, this mission; and if it is a mission, which I have been destined to complete, then I will achieve it."

"See, you later Amaroca." the Dogman yelled and left, simply vanished out of her sight.

Now she was alone and the light of the day became weaker until it gave way to the darkness of the night, which now was soon to encompass the forest. Stuck in the well and surrounded by strange energies, Amaroca commenced hearing weird voices, which were testing her spirit to the limit, by calling her names and humiliating her person. The voices seemed to know everything about her life and were at the beginning very intimidating to her.

Suddenly Amaroca fell into a strange slumber and just fell onto the floor, which was very moist and partly inundated by water. She was immediately caught in a dream world of utter obscurity and darkness, where she was haunted by beings, which she could not identify and could not see. She only could hear them breathing and chasing her through dark alleys, where no mortal soul had ever gone to. The hours went by and soon the night began to fade, but Amaroca was still in this world of dreams, which had completely encaptured her mind and soul. Still running from these beings, who were following through every corridor and street, which she was walking on, she came to the realization, that these beings, were just parts of her fear, embodiments of her own weaknesses, which were feeding off her own insecurity. So, she had the idea, of calling on the Great Spirit, the source of life and asked in her despair, for she did not know, at least at that moment in time, how long she still would have to linger in this horrible world of devilish nightmares, which was teeming with evil and strange beings, who were malevolent and full of malice. "Please help me light. Please help me God and tell me, what I should do." she cried, but at first, she could not hear any answer.

Then again, she cried, as she was enshrouded and surrounded by thousands of dark beings, who had now successfully managed to besiege her mentally and spiritually: "Please help! I will give my life to you if you help me! Don't you know, that I have a daughter, whom I love and who would be very sad if I were not to come ever again?"

In an instant, in a twinkle of the eye, a light appeared and expelled the hordes of dark beings, who had almost totally absorbed her soul. Then a stark and holy voice spoke to her: "Yes, I will help you, but you must forgive and love your foes. Forgive and you will be back home in a second as if nothing ever had happened." "Okay, I will try to forgive. Please help me to forgive, for some things, which have happened in my life, I cannot easily forgive," she replied in a meek voice.

"Good. I will give you the strength so that you can forgive!" the holy voice, coming from the light responded.

At once Amaroca had the capability of forgiving and forgave everyone, who had inflicted pain on her. "Very good girl, now you shall be back at your house in no time!" the voice said.

Before Amaroca noticed, she was lying on her bed and could hear the sweet voice of her daughter calling her. She looked at her clock and it "Was this just a bad dream, or was this really just happened?" she thought to herself, pondering about the events, which seemed so real to her.

But then, did it really matter, for was not the end, the final result of this experience, a good one?

And then she drew to the conclusion, during the latter part of the morning, that, that what she had recently experienced was real to here and that was all that mattered. Then an image of the Dogman appeared, whom she had encountered yesterday. She could see his brown fur and his yellow eyes glowing and his pointed canine teeth smirking and saying: "This was your first task and now we shall see if you are fit for the next one.

So, this is her story, albeit her first adventure with a creature, who appeared to her as a Dogman, a cryptid, who is still unknown to most in this part of the world. If Amarocas was a dream within a dream, as Edgar Allan Poe, used to say, is up to your reader. But for now, Amarocas journey ends and soon she might be tested again, to find out if she is capable of manifesting her destiny, as the light had designed it to be.

The End

The Dogman of Ouachita County

The beautiful mountain range of the Ozark Mountains is a joyous experience, which everyone will love. But these mountains have many secrets, which, if unraveled could cause fear amongst the locals and tourists, who venture into the pretty forests of this mountain range, which has majestic creeks, rivers, ponds, and gorgeous meadow. One could think, that if God or the universe were a painter then he would take a long time to paint the beauty of these mountains. This story took place in these mountains and I, being a fan of the forest for a long time, since I can remember, have spent many precious moments in the Ozark mountains, which I would not want to miss at all. But now, since I have encountered a creature, which I can only describe as a dogman, my perception has changed and my caution has gone up a notch, although I must admit, that my encounter was not so bad, and, who knows, maybe these dogmen aren't all vile creatures, perhaps they just want to be left alone. But this speculation is another story and a theme in its own right and own device. Now I would like to commence telling my personal encounter with the dogman, which was on a beautiful day in autumn, I think it must have been the fifth or seventh of November, for I recall, that it was quite chilly in the morning, when I started hiking near Roland, heading for the wonderful Lake

Maumelle. The day was sunny and I could hardly hear a bird singing in the forest. On this day, which I have named dogman day because this was the day, that had me a believer in this phenomenon. I also would like to mention, that I hardly met a fellow hiker on this day, and especially during the first hours of my hike, I could feel a great placidness, which had a touch or should I better say a shade of solitude. This day was one of these days, that could give a hiker the feeling of being totally alone and, if he was open-minded, in tune with the majestic prowess and beauty of nature. So it came to pass, that I stopped a few times before I arrived at the rear shore of Maumelle Lake, which was, especially on that day, a world of its own. The wonderful blue greyish color concoction of the lake fascinated my avid and curious mind, which was just full of the pioneer spirit and yearned for those days when there were just Indian tribes, cowboys and trappers. With this state of mind I gazed at the lake and showed my highest respect for its individual expression of the Ozark Mountains wide range of wondrous features of its unique being, if one would take into account, that the Ozark Mountains were a living and breathing creature of nature, which always had new things, new surprises for the open-minded and brave hiker, who felt like a mountaineer of the early 19th century. After enjoying the lake for a while, I decided to go further towards the Ouachita National Forest, which was about nine to ten miles away. There I wanted to visit the Lake Winona and camp there for a day or two. I really loved the mountainous foresty region of Ouachita National Forest.

But I actually never got there, because sometimes things don't turn out the way you planned them. As I was going further away from the man-made Lake Maumelle, I thought, that something or someone was following me. I was walking near the road, to maintain some sort of good orientation, in spite of knowing the region quite well. The first strange thing, that I can recall, which could have been associated with my experience with the dogman, was that I could clearly hear something moving fast, as I was walking from W Hundley road to Wilhite Branch through the forest and partly rugged country. The weird thing was, that this thing was keeping a good distance of about 200 yards, but still, I was able to hear it moving swiftly through this countryside. „Could this be a bear or some big deer? They don't come around so often or do they? But can they move that fast?" I thought, whilst emotions and feelings were encompassing my body and my mind.

A few minutes past until the fast or should I say very fast movements stopped. Now it was quiet again, but strangely enough very quiet, I would go as far to say, that it was unusually quiet for this part of the Ozark Mountains. I tried to clear my mind and didn't bother anymore to think about what it could have been, because I was just totally concentrating on my hike and had no intention of ruining the rest of my hike with worries and doubts, which only as a matter of fact would have destroyed my good spirit and my extremely good mood at that time.

So I walked in and after an hour entered Ouachita National Forest, which was beautiful and teeming with life. As I was wandering through the forest with awe and tranquility, I noticed, that something or someone was following me. The weird thing was, that I could feel the energy of this energy and it gave me a feeling of unease. At times I stopped and looked around because I wanted to know, who or what was persecuting me. What was going on? Was I imaging things, had I smoked too much of my weed in my youth, to hallucinate things like this? After thinking that I thought to have heard a snarling sound, which made me feel nervous, for I had not heard such a sound before, and trusts me, I have been in the woods and know a lot of animals and this sound was not at all familiar with me. Whilst thinking I totally forgot my surroundings and then I could suddenly feel the breath of a big animal, probably snorting behind me. I turned to see, what animal this could be and then I saw something dashing past me and I could only catch a glimpse of what it was. I was stunned for a moment and then I realized, that this animal was extremely fast. „What could this be? A bear doesn't run that fast nor a cougar?" I thought, starting to become worried and a bit distraught and decided to chill out for a while and just lie on the ground for a while. Lying on the ground, I gazed at the trees and the beauty of this forest, and my mind began to mitigate itself. Happiness seemed to return to my being and the queer experiences, I had just had, were gone: for now; I must say if I want to be correct because I will still expound on that, what happened only a few hours later. Time passed and I cannot exactly recall how I spent my time until I had my first real glance at this magnificent beast, that I did at the end not really perceive as a great threat, although I am sure, that there might be some of that kind, that might be really vile, who am I to judge.

As I was hiking and it must have been around 6 pm. Already, because I was already quite near lake Winona when I heard a growling noise of some sort. At first, I thought, that it might have been just some stray dog, but then when I had heard it again and again until it finally stopped, I commenced to think about the possibilities, that it might have something to do with the strange occurrences I had a few hours back. I was almost at the lake Winona and wanted to put up my tent on some nice spot, where I could enjoy the lake and the beautiful forest.

The moment I reached the lake and made myself a cozy little campfire and put up my tent. Then I remember, that I made the decision to lie down in the tent for a couple of hours, to relax and be at peace again with myself. This was so important for me then and now, for peace and stability are the pillars of a nice and fulfilled life, at least that is the way I see it.

After lying in the tent for a while strange things started happing. The first thing, that was strange is, that I could clearly see the shadow of a dog-like figure striding around my pretty tent. Then I could hear some snarling and growling and as I took a peek out of my tent, I could see something that was absolutely awesome in the true sense of the word.

Standing on the shore, about 40 to 50 yards away from my tent was a humungous creature, which after my estimate would be about 12 to 14 foot tall, but that is just a wild guess, because I was far enough from it, to not really be able to give a more precise estimate of its height. The creature had pointed ears and amber looking eyes. The creature was hairy and possessed a large snout. I think, that its fur must have been black with a brown undertone, but I am not really sure, because it was already quite dark and a bit after dusk.

After a while, I sensed, that it knew, that I was staring at it, and the strange thing was, that it did not focus on me gazing at it with total amazement and a dash of awe and haze.

The eyes, for me, were the most fascinating thing is possessed. For an instant, I thought, that these amber eyes, could change their color at will. I don't know what it was looking for, or what it was exactly doing at the shore of the pretty and in my point of view majestic Lake Winona, but I am now damn sure, that it could have easily killed me if it wished to.

This creature was just out of a horror movie, and I can understand, that it is hard to believe, that something like the dogman can exist in our so-called world of reason and logic. I know, that this all sounds pretty out of the ordinary, or totally berserk, but I am just saying and recalling, what I have experienced, and I challenge every doubter, to go out in the woods, or to the places, where they have been spotted multiple times, and experience an encounter for themselves, because I reckon, that one can only believe in such a thing, or let's say is a lot more probable to believe in the dogman, if one has met him eye to eye.

Then after about five to ten minutes, the dogman vanished, and if I say vanished, it really did, because it was gone form one moment to the next and that really astounded me, because now I know, that it was very probable, that this dogman had been following me or at least observing me.

After that everything was quiet and I fell asleep. I woke up quite early in the morning to the sound of birds chirping. I packed my tent and got all my stuff. Then I continued hiking for the next days, and I recall, that everything went fine and I spent a marvelous time in the Ouachita National Forest. Nothing strange happened again. Only the last day of my hike, when I was returning home on a little detour and on another route, I had another encounter with the dogman, probably this one, but who can really tell, because some of them look very similar and it was dark as I had it. The encounter must have been on some road, where I was hitchhiking because my car was at my house and my cell phone was not with me too, I had another encounter with the dogman. I am not sure which road I had the encounter, but I guess, that it probably was on Hot Springs Highway near Benton, lest I am confusing something. I think it was around 9 p.m. or maybe 10 p. m. and everything was quite. There was a cold breeze and I was hiking near the road and following it to Benton, where

I wanted to take a bus to Little Rock to a friend's house. Suddenly I had this feeling again as if someone or something was watching me and then a dogman appeared approximately 50 feet in front of me. It was a tall creature, perhaps 10 foot in height, and as I mentioned before, I am not sure if this one, was the same one, that I saw on the shore of Lake Winona. The dogman snarled and then just stared at me, as if it wanted to tell me something, and then something really weird happened. I thought, and now I think, I might have to really take this into account, that I heard a voice telling me to respect the dogman and not venture into the woods at night because that was the time when they were hunting. And now comes the really weird part, as the voice ceased talking to me, the dogman disappeared and I was truly intrigued.

Well, that is actually all that I have to say with regards to the dogman.

By the way I want to stress, that I never went into the forest at night again and since then I have never had another encounter with a dogman in Ouachita County or the state of Arkansas, although I am aware, that there have been and still are multiple sightings of them in the United States and the rest of the world. All I can say is that if you respect this creature, it will leave you alone most of the time; but of course, you should not be hiking during the night, because the nighttime is its hunting time. With that all said, I wish you all God's blessing and a wonderful time in Ouachita County if you happen to visit it.

The End

The giant Troll

Trolls have always been a part of Norway's culture and folklore, but rarely have real encounters been written down. Here is an account of a village's encounter with a mountain troll and this book, which I am about to open, will unfold the content of this interesting story. So, let me commence to read the tale of the mountain troll, who stalked a village and rampaged and ravaged through the nearby settlements of the village. So I dive into the story and begin to tell you a story, which I am convinced of being true, if not then at least very imaginative.

The fog lay thick over the village on a November day. The quiet hours of the morning had begun and gave a wrong impression of reality, the reality of the people of the early 18th century. The times were harsh and the life was simple. Most people knew, that the legends of the creatures, who were roaming through the mountains and sometimes resided in some remote cavern, were true. Many years had gone by since the people of the village of Hemstod had seen a mountain troll. A tall and fierce being of the times of old. A creature which partially resembled a man, but still had elements of a raging beast in him, let alone his attributes of cruelty and the evil dwelling in it, which surpassed the viciousness and vileness of most humans.

As the farmer by the name of Jorg woke up, he could hearken the thumping of feet walking past his pasture, which was adjacent to his little abode. Every step, which trod on the ground caused him to quiver. His wife Arma was still asleep and he had no intention of waking her, why should he? His mind so perturbed and vexed by these sounds, that his face turned pale and his eyes took on a shade of luminous grey. But he was not the only one, who would be scared by the terrible uncanny sounds of a creature, which for a long time, had not ventured into the territory of this region of Norway. The old fisher Jonstad was also having another one of his naps and realized as he was literally pulled out of his usual morning slumber by ominous cracks of the branches nearby. "My God, what on earth is this?" Johnstad asked terrified and paralyzed by fear, for he had never encountered such weird sounds, which made the earth around his house trepidation in such a way, that he at first thought, that he had just experienced an earthquake for the first time.

But something foretold him and soon thereafter the whole village, that this was no earthquake of any kind, but a beast, who had been awakened from its slumber.

Fear and anxiety were soon to spread throughout the whole village and everyone was alerted now. "This cannot be really happening, or is it? Could this be a giant of yore, a crude and brutal savage being, who kills and eats the flesh of man?" an old man, who was living in the center of the village and had been frightfully alarmed by the thumping footsteps, which were heading towards the little village.

The people, who were outside and going after their morning business, suddenly all hurried inside their homes and locked their doors. The streets were emptied soon and the sense of fear pervaded the normally quite harmonious atmosphere of the village. Carefully with an anxious look on their faces, some villagers peeked out their windows, to see whether the giant was now wandering the village streets, but the only thing, which was able to hearken, was the heavy treading of the giant's clumsy way of walking on the nearby forest paths. Then the giant stopped as it was about a few hundred yards from the village and let out a bloodcurdling roar, which caused some of the windows of the nearby houses to shatter. Soon after the roar had ended, footsteps were being heard again, but this time they had a much faster pace, than before. The giant stampeded into the village and swung its club wildly around, waiting to see, if it could randomly destroy a home. The stature and physical prowess of the giant were immense, for it towered at least 15 feet over the little 15 feet tall huts, which gave it an approximate height of around 30 feet. But not only its height was a menace, but also its gigantic mass of flesh and bone, which easily had the weight of five full-grown oxen. Eagerly and very vile it commenced to ravenously damage some houses, which were situated on the outskirts of the village. With great might and in a very cruel manner, it thrashed the rooves of several houses with its huge wooden clubs, which seemed to have some metal spikes attached to its end. Screaming and despair came from the houses, which had their rooves completely obliterated in a few minutes. The people inside hid under their beds and fled into the cellar, if they had one.

But then something extraordinary occurred. The fog, which had covered the village and the surrounding forests, began to fade and drift away, permitting the sun to shine its rays on the village. As soon as this took place, the giant troll commenced to stampede and fled out of the village in the blink of an eye into the vastness of the forest.

The giant troll had vanished, for now, leaving an aftermath of partly damaged streets and broken rooves, which could fall apart any minute from now. Silence environed the village again and the villagers regained some of their courage, because they knew, that the weather, the rays of the sun, had spared their lives and saved them from an unimaginable atrocious fate of being eaten alive or torn apart slowly and then being boiled in some cauldron, far away up in the mountains, where no one would hear their cries of sorrow and agony.

So, peace and harmony once again returned to the village, which was now quite concerned about the proper way of dealing with the repairs of their streets and the rooves of some of the houses, which had been strongly damaged. It took a while for the villagers to repair everything, that had been destroyed by this ravaging beast, who had now reappeared and made clear, that it would probably return again. But what should they do to successfully fend it off, if it was superior to them in every aspect of their being?

This is why the council of the village came to together, after the repairs had been almost finished and the sun almost faded away, leaving room for the darkness of night to sweep across their village.

"I think, that we should surround our village with torches and lanterns; maybe we should even make bonfires in every street and around every farmhouse. Perhaps these sources of light could be strong enough to scare it away for the meantime. But who knows what may really help, but I believe that these precautions are worth a try? Or does anyone here have a better idea?" the old council member Joran said. "Well, I think, that your plan of doing such a thing, is great and we support you. The council supports you. Let us create fires and light as many torches as we possibly can. What else can we do? Only fate and god will know if this good idea will really work out well." Björn the head of the council replied under heavy approval of the other members, who were delighted, that Joran had come to construe such an idea in his mind.

So, the council members informed all the villagers to gather up lots of wood and pile it around some places nearby the village and told them to kindle their torches. Steadily and fast the villagers did as the council told them to do and soon there were many fires burning around the village and many torches lit, which were stuck every then foot of the way of the streets into the firm and now damp ground. The village was soon very luminous and for now, the troll avoided the village, although it was still heard faintly wandering wildly and ruthlessly through the forests. Fear and anxiety were still in the hearts of most villagers and no one, except for the council members, was really convinced of this idea, which seemed like a stupid illogical whim to most. The hours went past and it did not take long until the first rays of the sun greeted the village, which was still lit by all these various sources of light.

Then as the morning was well on its way, the council member reassembled and decided to extinguish the fires during the day and commanded the villagers only to light the fires and torches at dusk. further on they pleaded them to use petroleum and oil lanterns, which should be another source of light, which in essence, should strengthen their incandescence.

The obedient villagers did, as they were told by the council, albeit more or less willingly. What other chance did they in fact have than to listen to the councils and its commands? Was there another choice of another option? Was there another cure, another remedy against this malevolent being of old, which was feared since the dawn of creation? How should they opt for, if not for the wisdom, the sages of the council, who almost never had made a bad decision in their lifetime, albeit of course sometimes have drawn some conclusions, which were bad and may have been solved in a better manner; but one shall not forget that the human mind errs, but the divine forgives.

The hours and the days went past and soon the village had been repaired and everything seemed to have come back to normal again. So, time flew and not for long the vestiges of the giant troll's destruction, were not visible anymore and if one had not experienced the damage and psychological agony oneself, one could have thought, that such a monster had never ventured into this village and not even touched one stem of its grass.

But, sadly this story doesn't end here, because after a few weeks had come to pass, steps and ferocious cries were heard, especially at night, although they seemed to be coming from a good distance away from the village. Some hunters, who dared to wander and hunt in the nearby forest, claimed to have seen the giant troll again and added, that it was not alone, but in the company of other, grimmer, trolls, which, according to their description were of a bigger build and a more monstrous stature.

"As I said, I have seen it and it was not far from the river, where we usually fish. And I tell you, my lads, it was surrounded by some more evil companions. I don't know, what is going on, I only know, that this can for sure is no good omen." the hunter Janson spoke, as he was modestly sipping his beer in the village tavern. "Na, I guess, that you must have been imagining something! Why should it be nearby, if we have taken measures, which seem to be so effective, that it has not to tread on our village grounds for the past three weeks? Come on Janson, you are getting yourself wound up again because you are just an old quaffer!" the tavern keeper replied. "No, you are mistaken, Trensip, has seen it too and he is no drunkard like me! Trust me, I have seen it and it is not alone!"

"Well, well maybe you are right in some way or another, but the troll is not coming back. Why should it? The trolls fear the sources of light and despise it because they turn into stone if they are exposed to it Janson, you should know, hasn't your mother told you that or have you not been to school!" the tavern keeper remarked with a harsh tone.

Outside the tavern, the light of day waned and the darkness of night commenced to sprawl across the Norwegian sky. A touch of solitude surrounded the village, which deemed itself to be secure, but if it knew what was coming, it would have trembled with anxiety and fear.

A few hours later as night had embedded the village and its surroundings, sounds of many thumping steps were heard. Some villagers, who were guarding the village, as the council had commanded them to do, perceived the presence of many big beings, who encircling them. Soon cries of this guards were hearkened; cries of despair and dread.

"My goodness, what is going on. Haven't we taken precautions? What is happening? Wake up the members of the council!" George the head of the council told his wife, who was lying next to him in his bed. His wife awoke by his admonishing words and looked at him like a startled animal and then after recovering from her state of bedazzlement, she answered shivering slightly: "Yes, George. Yes, I will warn the members. I will wake them up!" Quickly she stood up, got herself dressed and headed out the door of the head councils house, whilst George sounded the alarm bell, which was in his living room. In an instant, the village was alarmed and the feelings of terror once again pervaded the atmosphere, which had been so harmonious and beautiful for a while.

Like striking sounds of thunder, the giant troll's presence penetrated the wonderful starry night. This time it was in the company of other, bigger and viler trolls, who loved to eat the flesh of poor human farmers and mere mortals. Panic and fear spread quickly and the villagers were disappointed with the council's plans, but on the other hand, scared and full of despair. Without really knowing how to properly defend themselves, they hid under their beds and fled into the cellar, if they were in the possession of one. Only a few brave villagers faced the fierce trolls and died a horrible death, whilst trying to fend them off with burning torches. Their screams of agony and pain were heard throughout the whole village and everyone was petrified, as these brave villagers screamed their last words, which were a mix of blatant fear and resignation.

After annihilating the little resistance, that they encountered, they commenced to totally ruin the village. They tore down all the lanterns and completely destroyed all the rooves. Then they crushed the walls of all the village houses, which soon thereafter began to crumble and fell apart. The villagers, who hid under their beds, were now panting and trepidation with angst, they had never ever been confronted with in their lives of rural hardships. Soon the cries of the villagers were heard, who did not have a cellar to seek refuge in. The trolls just simply broke their beds in two and threw their parts around the whole village. Quickly they were able to grab the totally petrified villagers, who were cowering on the floors of their roofless houses and tucked them into their huge sachets, which they had brought with them.

"Good, good, we have some food now, let us go!" one of the giant trolls said, whilst smirking devilishly. "Yes, supper is always a good thing. Fee fa and fum, they smell good these little humans. We will enjoy every bit of them." another troll said. Then the troll, who had already once viciously attacked the village and seemed to be their leader spoke with the most deep and unpleasant voice, which one could imagine: "Yes, they will be our food for the meanwhile and we will take of the rest. Let us go now to my friends and prepare our meal!"

With footsteps, which caused every path of the village to quiver, the giant trolls sped off and ran into the darkness of the night, which had been witness to their folly and rampage. The other villagers, who had not been kidnapped by them, only to be a while later cooked and eaten by these horrible atrocious beings, took at least an hour to recover from their state of extreme shock and despair.

The council members, who all had survived the assault of the giant trolls, decided, that the villagers should abandon the village and take everything valuable with them. So it did not take a long time, until all the survivors, all the villagers, who were still living and breathing packed all their belongings and left the village with their horse- and ox-drawn carriages. Never looking back, they traveled many miles further south, until they found another place, which was next to another village, where they would settle down and build another village.

But still all the fear and the loss of many of their people, was present in their hearts and souls, which would be perturbed and vexed by the terrible events, which they had witnessed, whilst being subject to the anger and treacherousness of these beings, who are called the giant trolls of Norway — beasts of old, men of perdition, albeit creatures of an era of savage and malign demeanor. Creatures, which man should avoid at any cost, for he can never know, if he might be their next meal, their next flesh, which they consume, to satisfy their primitive and ravenous urge for delicious food, which for them are human beings, who nowadays don't even believe, that these giant trolls are real. So, beware when you venture too far up north into the forests of Norway because you never know whom or what you will meet there and that might entail, that you will never ever see the beauty of the day or your loved ones again. Hence take heed and beware of the Giant troll.

The End

The Mountaintroll of Alaska

The question arises, whether giants exist or not. For many centuries, maybe since the dawn of humankind, giants have been the subject of many tales and legends. But are they really only a myth, a made-up concept to scare children and frail old people? If one looks at the various reports of giant skeletons, which were found throughout the last centuries, then the probability is evoked, that there are some substance and indications to the bold statement, which claims that giants are as real as everything else, which we perceive to be real.

This story is the account of a mine worker, who came face to face with something, he could not even think of in his wildest dreams, because he until he had this first-hand experience, with one of the most terrifying cryptids, would not believe the tales of the natives, who had an oral tradition, which only dedicated itself to the different species of giants. Yes, reader, you have read well, there are, according to many Indian tribes, many different species of giants. It seems, that everything seems to come in a lush form and there is even a great multitude amongst the rarest species; perhaps they are Gods or plainly just natures design, who knows for sure, for we are not God, but mere mortal beings, at least most of us.

It was the year 1920 as Mr. Bevensen was working for a mining company, unaware of the risks, but probably the good salary had enticed him and lured him into taking that job offer, which really was a good catch for a middle-aged man of 45. Mr. Bevensen was working near Juneau and his report, his personal experiences, which probably preceded this encounter, that he had made with something, so horrible, albeit incredible, happened in the same year near his workplace. But let the man speak for himself, for no one can describe the being better than him.

Here are his diary and the entry, which he had made on that day of the 10th of October when he had stumbled across something so big and bipedal, that his whole world view crushed in the blink of an eye, but not only that happened. Because of this experience, Mr. Bevensen eventually lost his mind and spent the rest of his life in an asylum, the poor man, I must admit, but let me not beat around the bush any longer and read to you the entry of his diary, which he had kept from the year 1915 until 1920.

10th October 1920

Another day of work has begun in the mine, where I have been working for several years now. The hard work in the mine is really strenuous and had truly fatigued my body. I don't know how much longer I can bare working under these horrible conditions; considering, that my wage is not really good. But lately I must stay something worse is vexing my worried mind and it is not the work per se. Some strange things have been occurring the last days, which cannot be blamed on the common perks of my coworkers. There is something out there and I know it, I can feel it, and this day I could really feel its presence, which I cannot easily describe, but it is something, which is so out of this world to most, that I dare not speak of it in public, although I have the urge to do so, because the world should know, that they are amongst us, even if they mostly hide in the vast forests and mountains of this and probably other states.

I don't know exactly when I saw this beast, this giant, who should not exist according to conventional science. I just know, that I can remember the thundering footsteps of this thing, which was on some kind of rampage. I think, if I remember well, that I was working in the lower part of the mine as I could hear the thumping sounds, which I could not associate with anything, that should have been down there. For a moment or two, I was bedazzled and distressed.

Then as I ceased my work to check out, what was going on I saw two eyes and the vague shadowy silhouette of a creature, who seemed to have humanoid features, although at first, I could not really see it very well, because of the dim lights in the mine. The creature, this being was walking in one of the side corridors, but not standing straight, because of its humungous statue, which I had the blessing or should I say curse of seeing, as I had finished my work for the day. Then it simply vanished out of my sight, only to return later at a different location.

The strange thing was, that it did not seem to notice me or at least not be interested in me. Who knows how they tick?

Perhaps I was not the adequate prey for it; which I somehow can understand if I think of my frail stature and my unstable mind. This could also be the reason why, I am still here and writing down my personal experience with a giant troll, also known as a mountain giant, that probably spared my life for this reason, but still it managed to scare the living daylights out of me, which I will explain in great detail now.

I guess it must have been around six or seven, sadly I don't really keep an exact track of time, so I cannot really tell precisely, when I saw the mountain troll again, but I know, that I was on my way to my car, which was parked about a mile away from the mine. It was dark outside and quite chilly and I had this feeling, which I was not able to suppress. This feeling, this notion, that someone or something was watching my every move and step.

Prudently I tried to walk at a quite fast pace and focused my mind on getting to the car as fast as possible.

As I was about a half-mile or so away from my car and I could already see it in the distance, where some lantern posts were shining, I suddenly could hear loud footsteps coming from the side of the path. A shadow appeared amidst the tall trees and moved quickly towards me.

Then in the light of the moon, I think, that it was almost full moon on this day, I could see the image of a huge man, who had claws on his hands and fangs coming out of his mouth. This giant man, who probably was the same creature, whom I had encountered in the mine only a few hours prior, was standing near a tall cedar and gazing at me. He seemed to be holding a club or some sort of weapon.

After staring at me with his fierce eyes, which penetrated my entire soul, he began swinging his arm and approached me. I just stood and could not move any further, for fear had overtaken my being completely.

The giant stopped right in front of me and now I realized, that he must have been at least 20 feet tall. But not only his height was intimidating; no it was his strong physique and his evil demeanor, which thoroughly had bethralled my mind.

A while after the giant had directly confronted me and I had the pleasure of hearing his deep and violent breathing, he picked me up and took me to the place, where my car was parked. He thrust me on the ground and started to sniff at my body. "Not good. I don't like that kind of meat." his loud and deep voice roared. "Have to find some other meat, but maybe he is good for my children?" the giant continued, whilst tossing me around on the ground.

I was so scared, that I did not know what to do, but to pray to God above, that he would spare my life, just for this moment, because I did not want to leave my family, who would not believe, that I had been a victim to something, which they could not believe in. And actually, if I am honest, I don't blame them, because I also would not have believed in such a thing as a mountain giant, if I had not had had this terrible experience with one.

Then something totally unexpected happened and I cannot explain why, until this day, if I am being frank with you. The troll, this giant of a creature, was about to swing its club and crush my head to bits, but something kept it from doing so and soon I was about to find out why. The giant troll did not pay any more attention to me and was now staring at the lights of 10 cars, which had just arrived at the parking lot. Gunshots and screams were heard a minute or so after it had gone away from me and left me lying on the cold Alaskan ground, which was harsh and damp from the frosty soil.

I was lucky because some workers had arrived for the night shift. I think it must have been around thirty men, who immediately began shooting at the creature, who did not expect any company at all. I was still trembling and panting on the ground, while I could hear the roars of the giant troll and the blood-curdling death cries of some men, who died in the fight against the troll, which spared my life.

I don't know how long I was lying on the ground, but I believe, that I was taken by two men into a car, which looked like an ambulance. I guess, that some of the men had called an ambulance, after the fight with this ferocious beast, that cost the lives of seven men and left 10 wounded.

Later I found out, that the troll did not die, it was only severely wounded by some Tommy guns, which some of the workers happened to possess, because of some bear sightings, and had stowed them away in their cars, for some potential attacks of some wild animal.; but none of them was prepared for such an encounter, an encounter with a terrible giant-like man, who could easily survive the gunfire of multiple rifles. But as fate has it, the giant fled, pushing out the last cry of anguish and anger as it hurried back into the dark forest surrounding the parking lot.

I found myself in a hospital, where I am now writing down my personal experience, which had entailed the death of seven men, good men, who are still to be mourned. What grief and pain their families are going through, I honestly cannot imagine, but it must be terrible losing your beloved husband to such a beast, which most don't even believe to be real.

Well, I am the living proof, that it is, because I have already been checked by a psychologist and a psychiatrist and both are of the firm opinion, that I am not mentally deranged or hallucinating, although both cannot accept, that I had been almost killed by a mountain giant, which I call a mountain troll, because its face has the feature of some depictions of trolls, which I have seen in my childhood years, as I still was believing in fairy tales, which in fact are true.

Luckily I am feeling better and the doctor said, that I will be able to leave the hospital by tomorrow evening. I cannot tell you how glad I am, despite of the things, that have occurred, which will cause me to quit my job, because I don't ever again want to be in the presence of something so fierce, that most people cannot even imagine being true, not even in their wildest dreams.

So, this is my account and I hope, that the world will know, that fairy tales and myths are true, and the world is really not, what we believe it to be.

Here the entry ends and I honestly don't know what I should add to the finishing lines of Mr. Bevensen, which I could not have formulated in a better or more profound manner. Hence, I will finish this story with these final words of ambiguity and say, that you read may decide whether you would like to believe in the account of Mr. Bevensen or not, for I will not judge this man's experience by any means and leave this up to you.

The End

The Skinwalker

The sky was dark again and many stars were covered by the clouds. Nehune the old chief sat around a campfire and started telling tales of the skinwalker, a creature, who has haunted the Indians past for centuries. And many theories encompass this being. Is it a being from another dimension or a shaman, who haunts the sacred grounds after his death? Or maybe just a spontaneous mutation or symbiosis with an animal spirit. Who can really tell? Maybe there are many different kinds of skinwalkers. Who really knows, unless he is something more than human, but that is in itself a different question.

So, here my story begins with the words of my grandfather a real American, a true native of the lands of Arizona. "Time is like the wind, it always changes its direction, but it will never stop until it loses its strength, but when this occurs, no one knows, only the great spirit. These were the things, which I was thinking about when I was driving to see my uncle in Arizona, who lived in the desert, far away from the next town.

My uncle was maybe a very estranged individual, but I was very fond of him, for he too was very versed in many things— especially the myths and legends of our tribe, which has a connection with the theme of this story. Well, my encounter with this being, occurred when I was staying at my uncles place, sadly I cannot exactly recall when exactly I was staying at his place, probably the things, which then happened have traumatized me in such a way, that I have forgotten the exact day when I first encountered a skinwalker, but I guess, that it is not so important, because in truth I just want to share my personal experience with everyone, who has the ears to listen and realize, that there are many things, which are real, even if we deem them not to be real.

But maybe I should start the story, when I was driving, as I have already mentioned above, to my uncle. I actually thought, that I would just visit him for a couple of days and that everything would be just smooth; I would be so wrong about that. But the queer thing was, that there were strange things happening while I was driving on the road at about dusk, this is what I can remember when I reminisce about it. So, I was heading out to my uncle's hut from Phoenix, where I had a house at that time.

I think I must have arrived at his place at around 8 or 9 p.m., but I am not too sure. But the weird events, which took place on the last miles to my uncle's hut, were in fact, if I reflect about it, indeed very odd. For example, there was a strange man walking on that lonely desert road, who vanished, when I looked back to check, whether he was alright. Or an uncanny crow-like bird, who was perched on some post on some random petrol station, which I passed on the way. Or that eerie feeling of the sky, which was somehow hiding some evil, which I cannot explain to this day.

At first, these things made no sense to me of course, but later they would, because now I am convinced, that they somehow are interlinked with this skinwalker, a being, whom I don't really understand, although I have been studying for quite a while now.

As I arrived at my uncle's hut, I was surprised that he was not there, so I simply waited in my car, waiting for him to return. Time went past and I could feel something watching me, although I could not really tell who or what it was.

Then finally after three hours or perhaps more my I could see my uncle's car, a good old jeep, driving towards me. He stopped the car right next to mine and got out of the jeep and greeted me, but something was not quite right, something was out of the order and I shall explain to you in a moment, what I am getting at here.

I got out of my car and greeted him with a very friendly smile. "Hey, uncle how are you? How is life?" I said with a very happy tone in my voice.

My uncle just replied in a somber tone: "Hey boy, get inside. Let us not spend too much time out here. It is night and it is better if we get inside."

Quickly we both went inside and my uncle slammed the door shut and locked it. The atmosphere was strange and his cabin seemed to be cramped with a lot of stuff, that he had acquired the last weeks and days since I had seen him last.

"Come sit down. I'll make you some coffee. Might be a long night; there are uncanny things going on here and I fear to even mention them, but I must."

he spoke with a nervous voice. "Why? What has been going on?"

I said, wondering what really why my uncle was so perplexed or in some anxious state, which I could not really comprehend.

"Well, boy. The legends are true. There is a creature walking the desert and it is not a normal creature, it is naalddlooshii, or better known under the name "skinwalker". " he replied.

"A skinwalker? I thought, that a skinwalker was a being, a creature of myth to scare little children." I said.

"I can tell you, believe me, or not, that it is not a myth, it is as real as the air, that we breathe every day. And there is something more, that I must mention. The last weeks have been really eerie and a lot of cattle has been gone missing and some dead mutilated bodies had been found. The bodies had been mauled and they had scratch marks, which could not have been caused by a cougar, bear or coyote. Of course, the police will not believe in such a thing as the skinwalker, but I know and our people know, that it is genuine. This is the reason why I always lock my door and have my guns loaded; just to be sure of course."

my uncle explained with a scary tone in his voice.

Then all of a sudden, a yell penetrated the night. The yell was really unusual and blood-curdling and I began to believe him. "Have you heard that.

It could be nigh and I should get my guns." my uncle said slightly scared.

"I don't know? This yell was creepy, but was it really a skinwalker's yell." I answered. "Are you still doubting my words, nephew? Have you never listened to the old men of our tribe, who have been telling these stories, these legends since your birth? What has become of you? Are you totally blind? Are our ways, the ways of our tribe to you like a foreign land?" my uncle insisted in a grumpy and disgruntled voice. I sighed and then again, the silence surrounding me and my uncle was interrupted by another vicious yell, which was followed by growls galore. I looked at my uncle, who whispered: "Now you, believe me, right?" I thought for a moment and then replied: "Yes. I guess, that you are right, but what are we supposed to do now? Should we wait?"

After I had said these words, my uncle stared at me with his dark Indian eyes, which had seen a lot of pain and turmoil, which I probably could not really grasp. Then he said: "We will see. For now, we will just wait inside. Sometimes the skinwalker just wants to scare you, and sometimes it will challenge you if it sees, that you are someone, who is worthy to be challenged." "Good uncle. Thence let us wait, maybe this is the wiser choice, that we can make." I answered and began to jump into a world of dreams, where every tree and shrub outside appeared to me as a sinister creature, a hideous monster, lurking outside and waiting to devour its next victim, who had no clue, that he would be its prey.

The hours passed and soon it was past midnight. The moon shone onto the cabin and had something ominous about it, which I was not able to put into the words. But this energy, this presence, which was emanating from it, really shook my mind and caused me to tremble with fear, that until now had been unknown to me.

My uncle, who had been eagerly watching and observing the darkness encircling the cabin, had fallen asleep; let me alone in my realm of perception, which was commencing to distort my world of ideas and sentiments. Every moment turned into some form of eternity, which had its own individual aspects to it, which I could neither interpret nor understand.

I don't know, why but I could not sleep and strangely enough, I was feeling very awake and strong; to my great surprise. Everything seemed quiet and the moon was exuding more and more strangeness by the minute. And then suddenly out of nowhere, a very odd coyote appeared near a bush, which must have been about 200 feet away from the cabin. The queer thing was, that this coyote was walking bipedal and had a head, which slightly resembled the features of a man.

Totally struck with fear and anxiety I just gazed at it, not knowing at that time, that I had just seen a skinwalker, who had been checking out my uncle's cabin, only to sense, whether or not he would be the ideal prey for his insatiable lust for flesh. At first, I think: the skinwalker did not notice me and was not aware, that I had seen him, but then he stared at me with his evil and penetrating eyes, that had so much energy and power in them, that I was not able to handle; so, I quickly ceased to stare into his eyes and look sideways.

After that, I heard a scream, which tore my uncle out of his sleep and caused the whole cabin to trepidate. My uncle quickly grabbed his gun, but was still in such a haze, because his eyes were weary and his state was very bad. But then after the scream had faded into the darkness of the night, a very eerie silence crept upon us.

The tension grew and my uncle whispered to me: "Get yourself a gun, there's own in the draw, and don't forget to load it with some ammo. There must be some on my counter. It is near, I can feel that and I have no idea, what it wants, just that it is interested in one of us. This what I can sense."

Then my uncle went taciturn and silence pervaded the cabin. Slightly trepidating and anxious, I got a gun, a colt, out of the draw and loaded it with some ammo, which was lying on my uncle's counter. Just about at the time, when I wanted to sit down, I thought or at least had the feeling, that something just moved outside the cabin window of my uncle's kitchen, where my uncle was sitting and staring at the wall.

I quickly sat down on the chair next to my uncle and held the colt in my hand, shivering and feeling to urge to flee; but escape was no option, at least at this moment.

Then I heard scratching noises at the door, which caused me to almost panic, but luckily, I could maintain my countenance and remain calm, which was very difficult for me in this very strange and precarious situation.

Suddenly I heard a howl and then the window next to the door was smashed into pieces. There it was, this creature standing outside the window and giving us a fierce and malicious look. My uncle took his gun and fired a shot at it, which it seemed to dodge because it there as began to attack us with its giant claws, with which it tried to seize me. At first, I hesitated, but then I fired off some rounds with the colt, hitting it straight the skinwalker straight in the head with several bullets. The skinwalker cried out in agony and fled, only to come back a few minutes later. Meanwhile, my uncle had grabbed another gun, a shotgun, which he loaded with some bullets, that had a silvery tone.

As the skinwalker returned howling and snarling, he fired off five rounds at the skinwalker, which just smashed another window and was attempting to climb into the cabin. The skinwalker screamed again in pain and fled into the darkness, where we for a while could still hear its vicious and uncanny howls, which eventually vanished in the dark of the night. Although my uncle then tried to calm me down and kept telling me: "Rest assured. We got it good, and it is not coming back, for I have perceived, that we are a foe, which is too strong for it. And sooner or later it will find another victim, whom it will probably try to devour."

I was still in shock and could not sleep at all, for this experience had truly changed my perception of life and taught me a very bitter lesson, which I had avoided for the biggest part of my life; but now I was confronted with a thing, that I had recently mocked and derided and simply denied.

Therefore, I must say, that the old stories are true and that, what is mere fantasy and plain ludicrousness for most, is in fact as real as you and I. But I am absolutely aware, that most people, who read this story, will question my sanity and I can understand them very well, because I was one of them.

But seeing is believing, as the old saying goes. So, please don't judge people, for what they see, because you never know, what you might experience in the vast deserts and forests of Arizona and other states or even parts of the world; because the skinwalker is out there and searching for an ideal prey.

The End

The Tale of the Leprechaun

I still remember the words of the old folk telling

Me stories as a kid, about the leprechaun a monster, maybe even some sort

Of demon of lore, who can really say for sure. I can only say, that I want to

Share my personal experience with this being, who has been haunting the

Minds of the Irish culture for centuries or even since it has been brought

Into existence.

The legend goes, that a leprechaun will always search for gold, which it hides on the other side of the rainbow, where it likes to dwell; but sometimes it will look for gold in our world. Why this is so, I cannot really explain and it sometimes crosses my mind, that I don't, in fact, know a lot about this monster, that has been and still is feared by many: especially the superstitious folks, who even have signs, tokens, symbols engraved on their houses, to protect them from evil vengeful spirits such as banshees and sprites.

Well, I don't want to go off on a tangent, because I am fully aware, that there are so many things, which maybe could be interlinked with this being, called the "leprechaun", whom I had the pleasure of meeting one day, which will always stay in my memory until I have passed into the next world.

The day, that I encountered this malicious hideous creature, was the infamous Saint Patricks day, which I was celebrating of course as usual with my comrades. I think it must have been around 3 or maybe 4 p.m. when I left the City of Cork, to return to my house.

But on this day, I wanted to visit a good old friend, who had just purchased a new home.

This home was a mansion, which had been having many strange occurrences, which were unexplainable to him and the previous owners.

The drive to his house was a nice long drive, which let me see some of the mystical places of the Island of Eire, which I really am fond of. It was dusk or perhaps I should say almost dusk when my car rolled into his front porch and parked in front of this grey but majestic looking edifice, which had been a witness of an era, that had been already long forlorn.

My friend greeted me, as I exited my car and I immediately noticed, that something was bothering him. His face gave me the impression of a somber and sullenness, which he had never had. "Hey, nice to see ya. Please come in!" he said trying to be polite and easy-going. "Thanks for inviting me! Nice place you have here lad, although I must admit, that it is not my kind of taste." I replied with a jolly voice.

My friend led me to the front door, which was of green color and very wide and tall. He gently opened the door and I followed him through a beautiful hallway, which was full of paintings, furniture and other things, that represented or better said, reflected the history of this mansion. I followed him through quite a few chambers until he told me to sit down in a saloon, which was next to a very roomy kitchen.

"Please have a seat and feel at home. Would you like to have some tea?" he asked and pointed with his finger on an old table surrounded by even chairs. I sighed for a moment and then I answered delightfully and slightly exhausted after the intake of so many impressions of the various chambers, which I had wandered through with my friend, to finally settle down in the saloon: "Yes, sure. Any tea will do the job, so just serve me any tea, please!"

My friend, who had gone into the kitchen, confirmed my sentence in a polite and stark manner, which had a taint of worry in it: "Good. I'll brew you some special Irish tea then. This one has some sea tang in it, which gives it the extra spice, that can really light up your soul. You'll have it in just a sec." Whilst I was sitting and observing the saloon, that had a timeless touch to it and if it were not for some electronic gadgets, it could have easily been the ideal setting for a scene in the novel "Jane Eyre", which by the way is a great novel with a lot of emotional depth and complexity. My mind was now traveling into the past and I almost did not perceive my friend's return out of the kitchen with some scalding hot Irish tea, which now was pervading the table with its fragrance. I could smell all the nuances and notes of its spectrums flavor.

"Please enjoy!" my friend said with a slightly somber tone in his voice. "Thank you," I replied and drank some of the tea, which reminded me of some time, that I had spent up north, where I had stayed in a hut next to the sea, that always had a strong smell, that was very similar to the fragrance of that tea, which I just had tried.

After a while of a short silence, I commented: "That house is really nice and it is a genuine relict and vestige of the past." "Yes, that is correct, but there is something about the house, that is very strange and eerie." my friend replied. "Why is this so, if I may ask?" I asked, doubting, that the house could be connected with anything strange or queer. "Well, lad! This house has a curse and there is a being, a creature, who sometimes haunts it. This creature is a leprechaun, a demon or troll-like figure from another world, which loves to collect gold and silver. A very mischievous rascal, who can be very hideous and is able to commit heinous crimes, which are unimaginable for most. Most people, lad, will of course not believe in the myth of this being, but it is true, even if most will deny it." my friend explained.

I was dazzled, hearing that, what he had just said. "This could not be true or had I misheard the words, which my friend had just uttered in a very friendly and Irish manner. "Excuse me, did you just say, that a leprechaun is haunting this house, your house?" I asked, still perplex and totally startled. "Yes, a leprechaun," he replied swiftly without laughing. "Are you serious? A leprechaun is a being of myth and it simply cannot exist. It is a figure of folklore and fairy tales to scare kids, but not a real being." I countered. My friend gave me one of his stern and serious looks. Something about the way he was staring at me, made me doubt my words, for I was convinced now, that my friend was not kidding and totally convinced of a leprechaun haunting his house, albeit it visiting on some occasions.

"Well, I am deadly serious and these creatures have been around a long time before us and will be haunting this island long after we have been interred in our graves. But I can understand you, you a man of reason, who doubts everything about the paranormal. Only what we can measure and sense is real, am I right?" he replied slightly ironic. "Yes, that is my nature, but if you are so uptight about the leprechaun, maybe I will be prepared to change my worldview, if you show it to me, so I can experience it for myself," I added, still partly doubting my friend's belief in the leprechaun. "Okay, then stay the night if you dare and you will see it for yourself; but beware, it is a very hideous and treacherous creature. The leprechaun will play tricks on your mind and then he might even try to kill you. If you are fully aware of that, then you can rest assured, that you are going to be in for a very interesting or should I say frightening night." my friend stated.

"Good, deal! I'll stay the night, but I would like to sleep in one of your bedrooms; they have such a nice view you know." I answered, confirming my friend's indirect offer, which I later would resent, because I really had no clue what I was about to experience and it was nothing of the sort, that I had ever lived through in my life, which had had its shares of dire straits, which I am not going to expound upon now.

The hours passed and my friend had gotten someone to tidy one of his beautiful bedrooms, which had a nice view of his garden and the lush fields of Ireland's mystical beauty. How I loved and indulged in the green of the island, which really seemed to be greener than most parts of the world, which I had been able to travel throughout my life as a medical doctor, who had been involved in many countless projects; but what would happen, truly would change the way I perceived the world in general.

Soon the darkness swept across the sweat meadows encompassing my friend's little estate and a feeling of uncertainty commenced to touch my mind.

Doubts arose and I tried to suppress them as usual, for I was a man of science, not some deranged or perturbed wizard, who dedicated his life to folklore and superstitious creed.

I am not sure, when it exactly occurred, the moment, that I realized, that something or someone was watching me, lurking somewhere in the begotten night, which always exuded this forlorn attitude of hopelessness and despair, although it sometimes was full of pleasure and delight, albeit on the surface.

So, I who was perching now on my friend's gorgeous bed, which was next to a nice, but for my taste, a little too fancy bathroom, wondering about what was going to occur. As I was drifting in my thoughts and notions of former years, I thought for an instant, that I could hear the sound of footsteps echoing in the hall, which was adjacent to the bedroom. At first, of course, I ignored them, but then as the sounds of these footsteps returned again and again, until they ware clearly audible, the words of my friend evoked in my memory and I started to wonder, if my world of reason and science, was really everything, which could exist.

Then suddenly I heard knocking and banging against the bedroom's door, which caused me to lose my ease. Now my world was about to crumble, at least the world, which I had been used to for so long. From that moment on I was certain, that I was not the only one near my room, for my friend's room was quite far away from mine and I recalled, that he told me, what I forgot to mention in this story, that he would be out until late at night.

Hence, I checked my watch and realized, that it was around 10 p.m. and I was pretty sure, that I probably was the only one in the house, because I knew, that his staff normally left his house at around seven p.m. So, what or who was this? Then something so strange happened, which shook me to the core of my entire being. Out of nowhere, or that was at least my impression, a small figure of a man dressed in green garments appeared on the window sill and began jumping and laughing. Its hue was of a pale yellowish complexion and its hair were red.

But its face was very wrinkly and especially its green eyes, which stared at me for a moment after they swept across the room. Then something even stranger even more bizarre occurred. This figure, which, how I later found out, was a leprechaun, commenced to chant these words, which I will never forget, for they really still are haunting my dreams: "Ho, ho tonight I'll find some gold for my desire. And maybe even someone, whom I may confuse and trick, with one of my best tales of a ruse. Ha, ha, ha. Long live the being, whom they call and scorn, the old and vile leprechaun."

I trembled with fear and could not move; in spite of wanting to flee and escape from this little very malicious midget like being, who was exerting such an evil, that made my whole body's organism cease for a moment, or at least I had the impression, that it was so. Then the being sat right next to me and pulled out a dagger and held it against my neck. "Now my little man of science, will you share some of your gold with me. Don't worry I also will accept Pounds, Dollars, credit cards and silver. Come on lad, or should I cut your throat!" the leprechaun said in a very hideous tone. I sighed and could feel the leprechaun pressing the blade against my throat and was utterly scared, but my urge to live was greater, so I replied: "There must be some money in my purse, I'll give it to you if you promise to leave me alone." "We will see about that lad. Only if you have some gold, will I let you be." the leprechaun giggled.

I carefully took the purse out of my pocket, the right pocket of my trouser and, I must confess, halfheartedly gave him all my money and a gold coin, which I had acquired five years ago at an auction. The leprechaun leaped back towards the window and I was relieved. "Very, very nice. Let me count the money and let's see if this coin is made of real gold. You just have saved your life lad. For now, I will spare your life lad, but everyone, who ventures into my realm, will have to pay to stay. Hahaha!!" the leprechaun laughed and simply vanished.

I don't think, that I could sleep that night and my friend was right, although he did not tell me, that this creature was very cruel and greedy. Then a thought arose in my mind, that my friend had not been quite honest with me.

The hours passed and I decided to read a book about the history of Irish culture, which was lying on a shelf near the bed. I was really still in a very weird kind of mental state and my heart began to pound when I heard a sound, which came from outside, but the leprechaun was not to appear again, at least for that night.

The next day came and I was greeted by my friend, as I came down the stairs in the morning. My friend seemed to be as normal as usual, but still, there was something about him, which caused me to think. "Hi. You were right, the Leprechaun really exists. Sorry, for doubting your words." I said. My friend gave me a look and then replied: "Well, I warned you. But there is something, that I forgot to tell you. The Leprechaun loves gold and will kill for it. I hope, well I can see, that you must have given him something, or else we would not be still here, but a dead corpse lying in one of my bedrooms."

"I know and I am wondering, why you had left out this detail about the leprechaun because I could have been killed. Could you please explain this to me?" I added. My friend took on a frown and I could sense, that he was ashamed by my words, which seemed to touch and ache his soul. "I am sorry, but you never asked and that is why, I thought, that I did not want to bother you with that." my friend replied. "Excuse me, my life was at risk and it was only by pure luck or by the grace of God, that I had some money and a gold coin on me," I said quite unabashed. "Yes, you're right. I made a mistake, but it is not my fault, that this evil malicious creature is haunting my house and is constantly asking my guests to pay it money or gold if they want to continue on living." my friend blurted out. "Right. But you should have told me. I mean you were playing with my life or at least taking into account, that I could have died!" I growled. "What should I say, it was my mistake and it shall never happen again; but what should I do? I cannot stop this Leprechaun and furthermore, it sees this house as its home." my friend sighed. I could feel, that my friend really meant, what he had just said, sop I forgave him.

"But there must be something, that one can do? Perhaps we can barter with him and just give him enough gold so that he will leave your house for good. I have some gold reserves and perhaps this plan might work." I said, after calming myself down.

"Well, that might sound like a plan to me; but the Leprechaun does not appear every night, albeit at day sometimes. I don't know when it will reappear, but this really could work, considering the fact, that it really relishes in gold and loves it more than everything else."

"Okay. I'll go to the bank and get 50 gold bars. I'll come back and we will wait until it reappears. Is that a deal?" I asked with a slightly badly tempered voice.

"Deal. You go to the bank and I will wait here for you; hopefully it will work, for I must admit, that I am responsible for some deaths, which have occurred, because I believe, that this being has haunted and killed some of my guest, who obviously have not paid it." my friend uttered.

I was terrified by what my friend had just said, but I tried to remain calm and said quite jovially: "So, it shall be then. I'll go now. I'll call you when I've got the gold, okay? Soon it will be over and then this killing will stop. I'll help you now." I replied and went upstairs to get my phone and my key for my car, while my friend searched for some books about Celtic mythology, which also described the characters of the Leprechaun.

Time went by and I was driving now to the next bank, which was in a Village about 10 Kilometers away. I entered the bank and transferred enough money into the account of the bank to be able to pay for the 50 gold bars, which I luckily received after waiting for two hours. The other customers and the bank clerk were behaving in a strange manner and could not grasp, why I was needing so much money.

As I left the sky became cloudy and it began to rain. Perhaps this was already a token for what was to come. I returned to my friend' house and knocked on the door. But something told me, and I am not sure whether it was intuition or just a plain suggestive interpretation of reality, that I was being watched observed.

After a while, maybe five or ten minutes, my friend opened the door and greeted me. I entered his house, which seemed to be different and really stranger and odder, than before. "I got the gold," I said. My friend just sighed and responded: "Good. Let's go to my saloon upstairs and talk about it."

I followed him upstairs past my bedroom and down that hallway, which leads to a saloon, where I froze as I saw, who was sitting on one of the chairs in the wide and beautifully decorated salon.

"Please take a seat. I will be back soon." my friend said and left the saloon. I took a seat and was holding the bag of gold bars in my right hand and could not believe, that the Leprechaun was just sitting in the saloon in broad daylight. "O very good. You got me some gold lad. Let's see, how much have you brought for me?" the Leprechaun spoke in a hideous voice.

I shivered slightly at first and then I replied: "I will only give you the gold if you leave this house for good. I hope, that you are prepared to bargain."

"I bargain is always good, if it is not in vain and there is much to gain." the Leprechaun answered, whilst laughing. "Well, I have 50 gold bars and I think, that that is enough for you, to change your residence?"

"Give me the sack of gold, don't be so bold and then you may grow old." the Leprechaun cackled.

"Good, here is the sack of gold, but I want to have your word, that you will leave this house alone and go away," I muttered. "Let's see, let me count and then I will tell thee, what I think." the Leprechaun said, as I handed him the sack of gold. Greedily and ambitiously I commenced to count the 50 nuggets and soon after it had counted the nuggets, it answered: "Good, but I will choose, whom next I shall abuse." I looked at the green devilish eyes of the

Leprechaun and its wrinkled face, that more resembled a monster than anything human or dwarflike.

"Yes, then where would you like to live?" I asked. The Leprechaun smirked and spoke: "Well, is this so hard a question to solve if you are the one, whose home shall be my utmost abode and grove."

I was petrified, but realized, that I had no other choice than to say yes because I wanted the murders to stop and thought, that I could somehow barter with this vicious cunning being of old.

"Okay. You can stay at my place, but I don't want you to kill anymore. Is that understood." I stated. The Leprechaun stared at me and tried to intimidate me with its malicious eyes, which were flickering and full of lust and greed.

"Well, then you must give me more gold and give me gold every year." the Leprechaun told me. "How much more and much every year?" I questioned him, hoping, that it would not be too much. "Hmm. Let ponder never wander. I guess, that one more bag of 50 gold bars and every year some twenty nuggets would be fine; because then I'll be to you and your own guest divine.

"Deal." I half-heartedly replied, knowing, that this would financially encumber my life; although I knew, that I was neither insolvent nor poor.

But truly this deal paved the way for a more modest life, because the gold, which the Leprechaun demanded really had a toll on me and my family's financial liberty.

Since then many years have passed and the Leprechaun has not broken his promise; maybe this is the price, that I had to pay and maybe a more modest and humbler lifestyle, is the way, that creation, God, life as a whole, had planned it for me.

Well, this is the tale of the Leprechaun and my personal story with it, which still continues on to this day, because I still have to pay it 20 Nuggets every year on the 17th of March — the day of Saint Patrick. Perhaps you should take this story as a warning and be aware, that you might not be so lucky as I was and truly start to believe, that the tale of the Leprechaun is as real as you and I.

The End

The Troll

Many stories have been told about trolls and many still believe, that trolls are beings of myth and that they are just a being of fantasy. Well, this story tells my personal experience with one and I know, that it is hard to grasp, because conventional science still teaches us, that a thing such as a troll is just a product of our human fantasy albeit a part of the collective human mind.

But then the question pops up, that spirit and mind might be two aspects of the same. For what is consciousness, if not the expression of life in every form and being. Can we not reason without doubt, can we not think of what is and not is, but even if a troll does not exist, does it not still exist on some plane, even if it is only a figure a part of an individual mind expressing its thought-forms in its own world, its own fantasy world?

Well I assume, that I am being too philosophical now and this was actually not my purpose, I just want to tell what I have experienced and what I have learned to be true, at least in my own perceived form of reality. Maybe I am wrong and maybe my experience was just a trick of my mind, an illusion, which I have created to cope with life's hardships. Well, reader perhaps you should read this story with an open mind and judge it after you have heard, what

I have to say because it might be interesting to discover if it maybe could be true, that such a thing as a troll could exist. Perhaps your reader should forget your predefined judgments and opinions of life and just listen to, what I am about to share with you.

Now let me commence the story about a strange creature, which I have met in a town not far from Hartford, the capital of Connecticut, where rumors of these beings have existed for ages. They just were not called trolls but little people or dark elves. So the name does not really play a major role, because the creature still remains the same creature, the same phenomenon, which has been perceived by many thousands of people throughout the ages of time.

Where the trolls come from and who really made them, is another question, which I will not address in this story, which is about to unfold. Now I will commence my story about my experience, that I had with a troll, who transformed some of my beliefs, which were shattered as I realized, that something like a troll was as real as an animal in the forest or the rain in the morning.

And now as I reminisce on my encounter with the troll, I try to ponder about my world of notions, of thoughts, which until I discovered the world of trolls, was utterly different compared to the possibilities of that, what we call „reality". So let me start to describe the day, which changed the perception of my life and left me somehow in the lurch in the new reality, which was forged because of this life-changing experience. It was a day in June, I think, but I am not quite sure, it was the 10th of June and I was driving from Hartford on the 44, to a nearby town called

Torrington, where my nephew was having some strange hallucinations, well that is the way I thought back then.

No wonder for a studied psychologist like I, a man of reason, and convinced of the materialistic concept of science, which already at that time had been refuted by the results of quantum physics, but that is another story. It was a nice morning and the sunny day forebode a beautiful day, which it really turned out to be.

I was listening to some beautiful Cantatas of Bach and had a book on psychological studies next to the driver's seat. I was indulging into the gorgeous music of the genius of Bach, whilst thinking of the weird imaginations of my nephew, who was eight at the time. What is wrong with my nephew? Is he traumatized and trying to project his traumas into a world of fantasy or is he just projecting them subconsciously into his own reality?

After delving into these thoughts for a while, I noticed a road sign, which read "10 Miles to Canton". Soon I would be there, only about another twenty minutes to the house of my sister, where my little nephew lived. Excitement surrounded my astute mind and I was suddenly in a kind of state of mind, that even I as a psychologist couldn't explain. I passed the last suburbs of Hartford and soon entered the countryside, which was a forest region.

It did not take long for me to cross the Farmington River and drive through the little town of Avon. Everything seemed to be quite calm and there was rarely oncoming traffic. After passing Avon, I felt as if I were diving into another dimension. Even at the point of my story, I could feel some veil between Avon and Canton.

After a short while I reached Canton and slowed down my driving speed, to make a turn into Cherry Brook Road, which was a bit outside of Canton, then after a short while I made a right onto Morgan Road, which leads through some rural area surrounded by trees and some paddocks, that must have seen better days.

Well maybe for everyone the past is the so-called "better days" because out of my experience, almost all of my clients loved their good old days, where everything was better. But was it really better or just individually better for them in some way? After pondering about this "good old days" phenomenon, I realized, that I was almost there and tension grew inside my state of being, which must have been a concoction of excitement, uncertainty and subconscious fear of the unknown. "How has my nephew been? Was he all right? Did he have another seizure or was everything okay with him?" I thought whilst concentrating on the road and looking out for my sister's house, which was sometimes not so easy to find.

As I came to the end of Morgan Road, I made a turn to the left into Olson Road, which would lead me straight to my sister's house. As I arrived in her driveway, I felt some somber tone in the atmosphere, which I at that time would describe as some sort of hallucinatory subconscious sensation. I left my car and turned off my music, which was on a tape that I took out and chucked into my jacket.

Then I locked my car and stood in front of my sister's house for a while, looking at its architecture, which was quite interesting, because it was an old farmhouse from the nineteenth century. Then I rang the bell of my sister's door and waited until someone, probably she would open the door. This instant of waiting, as I realize now, and I actually do not know why seemed to me like an eternity.

That was really strange, for I was and still to some extent am, a very time orientated person. But sooner I would have the grace, or maybe experience or however you want to formulate it, to meet this creature, which would for sure shock my world view and changes everything. Still, in my world of thoughts, which were strongly influenced by conventional science it's a strange rationale, I was bamboozled and in some kind of haze as a woman opened the door, which I at my first glance mistook for my sister.

I cannot explain why this happened, it is just the mere fact, that it occurred for a second, and then I noticed that this woman had nothing in common with my sister. "Can I help you sir?" the woman asked with her dark eyes and her pale complexion, which reminded me of some sort of ice cream blend, which I still cannot remember, just that I saw an ice cream at one occasion, whilst going for a walk with a patient, which had the same color as the skin tone of this woman, which just had opened the door to my sister's house. "Yes, I am here to see Sara Friedman. I would like to talk to her, it is a private matter concerning her family." I said, after being quiet for a few seconds, because somehow I was out of my intellectual equilibrium for a moment or two. "Okay sir and your name is?" the woman asked, "Well my name is Jacob Arwin, her brother. Could you please let me in?" I answered, trying to be polite, but still stressing the urgency of my visit. "Come in sir, Sara Friedman, will be with you shortly." the woman said and let me in the house, which always was good for a surprise, for

Sara always had a tendency to buy new furniture every five years or so. I don't know why actually, perhaps it was her way of coping with her situation; I guess the divorce and my nephew's state of mind in the last three years must have encumbered her poor soul. But let me carry on with the story, which is about to become interesting for various reasons.

As I entered the house, I could feel something, which I still can't really describe, but I am sure now, that it was the same feeling, which I had had outside the house and whilst driving on the road past Canton. It was this feeling which seemed to freeze time, keep it in some kind of eternal trance, as if it were a total illusion, even on this three dimensional plane, because even I as a psychologist knew, that it was very probable, that time did not exist in some dimensions albeit a lot slower.

It did not take long for Sara to greet me in the living room, where I had taken a seat on a chair, which had seen many decades and some repairs. It was a wooden chair and made out of some kind of oak that is almost extinct. Sara was in a mess, as far as I could tell and asked me about my trip and my day.

I told her, that everything was fine and that I had made some spare time to help her son. "Let me tell you about David's mental state. David, as you know, has been suffering from nightmares and some strange seizures; this is why I have hired a nurse to take care of him. Her name is Tracy by the way and she is good at her job. But let me tell you a bit more about David's latest mental state. For the last days, he is telling me, that a troll, who can change time and freezes his body, if he does not obey him, has frequented him. I know, that this sounds very crazy to you, but David is absolutely convinced of this troll's existence. The only thing, that I can say to this story is that some weird things have been happening in the last days and I actually cannot explain these strange occurrences, which manifest themselves in eerie noises, sounds, and queer odors." Sara explained. "Okay, calm down, I'll see to him if it is okay with you. I will talk to him and find out which thing is really bothering him. I presume it to be some kind of traumatic experience, which has caused auto-suggestive reactions in his subconscious mind. No worries, I can help him, I am a psychologist, I deal with this kind of stuff every day." I answered boastfully and not really knowing what I would go up against. Sara sighed and some relief came out of her, at least that was my impression. "Okay, let's go to David and you talk to him and try to analyze the situation. I'll be upstairs okay and if anything happens, please tell me," she said. "Okay, no problem, I'll inform you, if anything should happen, but trust me, I can deal with his problems," I responded and followed her to David's room, which was next to the aisle, not far from the living room.

On my way to his room, I could again feel this strange feeling enshrouding my emotions and my mind, which caused some bewilderment in me, but only for a short while. As we came to David's door, I heard some footsteps moving quickly, and then they suddenly stopped. Sara knocked on the door and said: "David your uncle is here to see you, please open the door.

The door opened and David was standing in front of us. He seemed pale and frail. I could see that his mental state was not so good; in fact, I would say it was very unstable. "Come in, and let me tell you what is going on. But please come in without mama, he does not like woman of a ripe age." David uttered. Totally vexed by David's words I told Sara quietly not to join us and leave me alone with him, she nodded and replied, that she would go upstairs now. I entered David's room and closed the door behind me. David went back to his bed and sat down on it. His room was quite small but full of interesting objects, which Sara must have bought for him in the last while. "Okay David, so where should I sit?" I asked curiously.

David showed me a place, where I should sit and replied: "Please sit on the floor, the chairs are reserved for him and his people." "Okay," I said, wondering who he and they were. "So tell me, David, what is wrong with you? What has been happening in the last days? Your mom seems to be worried about you. Remember David I am a psychologist and you can tell me everything, so just go ahead okay." I explained to David, who was listening to me astutely. "Well, uncle Jacob, I am feeling okay, but this troll and his servants are very demanding and that is why I am having nightmares. You must know, that this troll called Eddy really likes this house, he just doesn't like older women, especially the kind of woman that my mom incorporates. I hope you can understand, that this is the reason why I only want to talk to you or someone like you." David spoke.

"Okay, so can you please tell me more about this Eddy and his servants? Where do they live and what are they? And where do they come from?" I asked in a calm voice. "Well Eddy is a troll and his servants are little trolls, who help him do things. Eddy is a troll king, who lives next to the house in another dimension underground, but he wants to manifest himself more in this world because he likes its beauty. Sadly Eddy doesn't like some older female women, because they have an odor, which he cannot bear. Eddy is my friend and I have known him for a while now, sometimes he comes at night and sometimes in the early morning. He is especially fond of my room and likes to play a lot." "Okay so Eddy is a troll king and has little troll servants and they live in another dimension next to the house. David, what else can you tell me, does he only come at these times of the day or are their exceptions to this rule?" I asked, still not believing a word that he had said. "Eddy can come as he wishes, it is just, that these times are his favorite times, because of special constellations of the day. At this time he has more power and vital energy." David answered.

"Okay, so if Eddy can come as he likes, could you call him for me, please. I would really like to get to know him?" A moment of silence befell us and then David responded with a quiet tone in his voice: "He has just been here, just before you came inside. But now I guess he is busy, perhaps you should come later. I am sure, that he would like to meet you, but be warned, he will punish anyone, who mocks his existence. Eddy does not like to be called a product of my fantasy. Is that understood?" "Okay, then I will come back later and meet Eddy," I said, stood up and left David's room.

This was really starting to get off the hook because I was on the fringe to lose my own mind. The noises, which I had heard, before entering David's room were quite odd, and he believed them to be Eddy's.

And this gave me the creeps, although I at that time still thought, that David's was imaging things to be real and suffering under some kind of posttraumatic auto suggestive disorder, which made him believe, that he could see and talk to a so-called "king troll" and little trolls. In some cases, which I have heard of, this could be the case, but was it really the case with David? This thought and other notions haunted my mind for the next hours, as I decided to stay in the living room, write down notes about my talk with David and do some research on these rare cases, which I at that point had not had a lot of experience with.

As I was totally indulged in my research, I suddenly heard Sara's voice in the distance. Then an instant later her voice was closer and more audible and then I realized, that I was eavesdropping a conversation between Sara and Tracy. "Tracy, sorry to disturb you, but have you seen David? I have been looking for him for 10 minutes now and cannot find him." Sara asked Tracy, who then responded: "No, the last time I saw him, was when your brother called by." "Okay Tracy, could you please help me look for him and if we can't find him, we will talk to Jacob, my brother, and ask him for some advice." "No problem madam, I will help you, so where should we start looking? Perhaps he went outside?" Then Sara's voice and Tracy's voice faded away like an echo in a silent valley. But as it would turn out, I would not be unbothered for long, because what would happen next, not only gave me the creeps but turned my whole world view around and gave me a taste, of that what David was experiencing.

Suddenly I could feel something run past my chair and the table, where I had put my laptop on. Then after an instant or two, I could see a small figure dashing past me again. I caught a short glimpse of it with my right eye and this figure was strange because I had never seen such a thing. Then the figure dashed past me again and again, and finally, it jumped over me and on to the next window, which was about 15 feet away from me. It was really fast, and I was astounded because I had never seen something move so swiftly and apace. Then I could see, after looking around, that it was hiding behind the curtains next to the window, with the beautiful ornaments, because I could see them moving; one of the windows by the way, which Sara did not exchange

What on earth was this thing? A mixture of amazement and utter haze with a dash of fear enshrouded my whole mind now. Were David right and I a naïve fool, who denied everything, which was outside of our normal perception? Was it us, me, who was sick, because we denied these realities, trying to build senseless castles in the air, albeit create our own comfort zone, which in fact would not lead us anywhere. Wow, this was quite some experience and these thoughts, notions, were only the start of the mountain of reflection of our own reality and perception, which I had to surmount now.

But then something happened, that made the whole situation even more surreal. The figure came out of the curtains and appeared right in front of me. "Got you, you doctors think, we don't exist. Well here is the proof that we do. Not only we exist, but there are also many other creatures, who live around your doctor, that you aren't even aware of. You silly materialistic doctor, you stupid semi-intellectual moron, who believes, that he can cure his patients, by prescribing them medicine, which in most cases aggravates their situation. Welcome to reality doc, the world is more complex, than you have imagined. And by the way, doc, if you interfere in my relationship with David, you will suffer doc. Then I will have to punish you doc, I hope you understand."

Now I was in total shock, but also quite disgruntled. This figure, this troll, I guess, that is what one would call had just insulted my intelligence and mocked my way of seeing the world. Something, call it intuition, call it gut feeling, told me to stay calm and that is what I did, for a while at least and then I glared at this troll, which had grabbed one of my books and poked its weird nose into it, and said: "Okay, thank you for making yourself clear. I guess, that you are a troll, and that may be the reason, why I have had difficulties believing in such a thing, for the simple explanation, that I have never had the luck of seeing one, which of course does not signify, that such things as trolls don't exist. Perhaps you would like to introduce yourself and tell me more about your world. I would be glad if could learn more about you and your kind, maybe I could also help you with some problems, as you already know I am a psychologist."

The words, that I had just uttered, I regret now, because what happened then was very uncomfortable and I hope, that I can remember all the details because I have surely expulsed some of them.

After I had said this sentence, as I clearly recall now, the troll grabbed my throat and looked at me with his fierce eyes and then the room turned utterly black, as if it were night, but the darkness was coming from him, from his being or his mental powers, but it doesn't really matter, because both of these possibilities seem to coincide at one point or another. "You mere mortal scum, you should not have said that now I will punish you. Now you will suffer and your whole family and kindred will pay for what you have just said. I guess, that you don't really know what kind of troll I am and what kind of powers I possess." the troll blurted out filled with anger and hate. His tight grip on my throat didn't loosen and I thought, that I would die any moment, for I was already choking and gasping for air.

After a moment though he let go of me and threw me out of my chair unto the ground. I was petrified because I had clearly underestimated his strength and mental prowess. The darkness didn't fade it just took on some different shades and forms and all of a sudden I was surrounded by trolls and strangely enough I noticed, that I was not in the living room anymore, but in a dark moist cave of some sort. David was lying next to me with a gag in his mouth and whining. But I could also hear the voice of Tracy and Sara close by. O my, what a horror this was. The trolls were not only real, but they were, at least these, which I had the pleasure to meet, vile creatures and full of greed and vengeance.

The troll appeared right in front of me again, wearing a crown on his head and shouting out loud, whilst the other trolls, which I could see were jeering and gnashing their sharp teeth: "Which one should we sacrifice first to our god. This one or maybe this one, or perhaps this stupid psychologist, who believes, that he is superior to me, to me, who is a troll king, reigning over this area for millennia. What do you think my trolls, what do think? Should it be David, Sara, Tracy or this Mr. Jacob Arwin? You decide now my little trolls!" the troll king said pointing at me, at David and at Sara and Tracy, whom I could see now, lying not far from me.

For a moment every one of the hundreds of trolls, which watched all of us, turned silent and the troll king distanced himself from me, waiting in the darkness in front of me and sitting on some kind of throne, which I could only see vaguely, because of the darkness, which was only lit by some candles, that I had never ever seen in my whole life.

Then a multitude of voices screamed: "Jacob Arwin should be our next victim. Sacrifice him now my idle king!" The king came towards me again with ten other trolls, who took me and lifted me up, as if I were light as a feather. They were chanting strange songs, while they were carrying me into a room, which must have been next to the cave room, were I and the others were lying. The room was full of pentagrams and other bizarre occult objects. There was a huge hexagram in the center of the room and a table was standing in the middle of it. There were daggers lying on the table and an old book was lying on one side of the table, which was quite large. They put me on the table, still chanting and mumbling things, which I could not understand, and the troll king picked up the book and started to read some of its pages. The room, which was lit with a strange reddish light, started to change its appearance, and after a while, something started to appear in it. First, it was just a shadow and then I could clearly see the images of a demon-like being, which had the features of a troll but was just a lot bigger in size than me and the little trolls. This being was huge and it began to touch and smell my body. Plain evil was coming from it and I started to scream: "O God, I know, that I am a sinner, but please forgive me for denying your majesty. Please help me Lord, shine your light on this darkness!" "No god can help you now, it is too late Jacob Arwin! To late!" the being replied, but that did not keep me from screaming to god, who did answer, and this is the reason why I am still here and able to tell you my experience with this troll king, his trolls and this demon, who probably was a troll demon, if something like that should exist. What happened then was truly a miracle, for suddenly a huge light appeared, that was so bright, that all the trolls, who were about to kill me with the daggers, that I had seen on the table, were blinded and fled. Even the troll king and the demonic being disappeared, the just vanished, and the whole cave was now as bright as a sunny cloudless day.

I stood up and went to David, Tracy, and Sara and untied their fetters, which were made of some sort of cloth, which was not and still is not known to me. After untying them I took out their gags and said: "Come let's go, we have to go know." After that, I could see a path leading out of the cave.

The cave started to crumble and I could feel every inch of it shaking, I guess, that the light must have caused that, but that is actually a different matter, and not so important. I, David, Sara, and Tracy managed to flee out of the cave and hurried back to the house, which was about half a mile away. Shortly after leaving the cave, we could see and hear how it crumbled and collapsed. In an instant, the entrance to the cave was covered with loads of debris and heaps of rocks and earth.

When we came to the house everything was fine and I never ever had these strange feelings again, but now I was aware, that darkness existed, darkness which I had come across in the form of a troll king, a demon troll and their minions.

But thankfully enough I also realized, that the light of God was stronger than every darkness and that a humble heart could enable it to do miracles. So this is the end of my story and I hope, that you will never have an encounter with a troll, because who knows, maybe you will never live to tell the tale.

The End

The Yowie

Welcome to the jungles and deserts of down under. Welcome to the great southern land, which some call the biggest island and some the smallest continent. Well, I think it doesn't really matter, who might be correct, the fact is, that this beautiful land is now known under the name „Australia" and I am proud to be an Australian, blessed with a good and peaceful life and a wonderful wife and three great kids. I must say, that in fact, until I met this being, which for me is more a beast than anything else, my life was pretty and to most extent smooth.

There was never any experience with anything, which I would call unusual. By the way, I would like to state, that I was never a believer of any form of phenomena: be it paranormal or belief in mythical creatures. Perhaps I should tell you a bit about my hometown, which is not very far from the marvelous city of Melbourne.

Although, when I think of all these things now, I have heard of people gone missing in the northern part of the Yarra Ranges and the Blue Mountains. I was born and raised in Healesville, which is a few miles outside of the outskirts of Melbourne. And to be honest, I have never heard of the yowie, until I came across some aborigine guy, who told me about this creature, which I at first denied.

„You must be joking mate, there is no such thing as a yowie and I am absolutely convinced of that. The yowie is just some fairy tale, that the tribes believe in. I can also tell you why I see this that way because we as humans tend to create forms of belief to cope with the hardships of life, that is all it really is when it comes down to the truth. Please start to become rational and just accept, that the yowie is just a figment of your people's imagination, that is all it is!" I said to him. I remember, that he had a sullen look on his face and then replied: „My friend, I say this with all respect and honor, but you are wrong. The yowie is a creature, which has been seen throughout the ages of time and many people have already encountered this creature, so please don't judge something, that you cannot comprehend.

I also must add with all respect of course, that you have not been out in the outback or the forests, so who are you to say, that it doesn't exist. Are you the creator of everything, are you God?" „No, of course not, but I don't really believe in God, I think, that it is us, who are or have a spark of the divine in us. I am sorry, but I just can't be of the same opinion as you!" I answered and now I regret that, because I know, that I had offended my old friend, who for sure had a lot of knowledge oft he outbacks and other things, which I frankly just denied, because I, and now I admit it, was too much in my comfort zone at that time.

But sooner than later I would find out, that he was right all along. And how this came to pass I will tell you now and it had to do with my profession, which would play some sort of role in the Yarra Ranges. As a studied geologist and alpinist, I was asked to do some analysis of a mountain, well actually it was just a hill, close to the Yarra Ranges. I remember, that it must have been a day in may because it was not that warm and it was rainy.

My job would be to analyze the hill near Woodspoint and study the earth, do to suspicion of acid rain. I had no clue whatsoever, that this job would be a hell of a ride into an unknown abyss of having to be confronted with a beast, I until then believed to be a myth, not more than some stupid imagined fairy tale.

My whole perception of life was about to change and did not know, that I was so wrong about many things because once you see a Yowie, it is like realizing, that death is an illusion. I think you know, what I want to express with that. It is just so awe-striking and out of this world, that you just cannot live your life the way you used to live it. Why this is so, I will tell you at the end of my encounter, with one of the most ferocious creatures of planet earth. But let me first describe my road trip to the Yarra Ranges, which was quite interesting, because I had two aboriginal guides, who wanted to visit some sacred ground, something which was of value for their tradition.

These guides were appointed to me, because my friend, who was an aborigine, wanted, that they should come with me. He thought, that I could need some sort of protection, for he had had a dream, which was about a yowie and me. Of course, I did not take him seriously, but diplomatic as I was, I gave in and told him: „Ok, Sam I'll take your friends Jake and Mebra with me." These are the last words, that I uttered towards him if I remember correctly. Then I drove into the forest past some little towns and the trip went fine and I drove around the Yarra Ranges and ended up on Warburton Woodspoint road. There was so much lush green and all the trees seemed to glow on this day. Maybe it was the sunny day, which turned them into some kind of oasis, which covered the gloom that I would encounter shortly. Somewhere on this road we stopped the car and parked it because my first mission was to walk up to the top of a slope near Dungaree Creek.

The walk was quite steep and strenuous, but when we got all our gear on top of the slope, we were rewarded with the magnificent view, which cannot be put into words, because it had to be perceived, to be cherished. This is why I don't want to put my emphasis on it, but on the things, which were to happen soon after. After we had built our tent and made a nice little campfire, we started to hear something. Jake and Mebra were a bit at unease and told me, that they could feel something big lurking in the woods beneath us and around us. I told them, that they might be exaggerating, but then I could also hearken something, which sounded very unfamiliar to me. I must admit though, that I am not a ranger and I don't know many animals, but these sounds were somehow out of this world, that is all I can say.

Now I believe, that this was the first experience which I had made with this being, which most call Yowie. But I don't know for sure, so I am going to try not to be obsessed with this assumption. About an hour later or so, as I was checking if my instruments were okay, I could see a hairy looking creature not too far from me. Perhaps it was about 30 to 40 meters away from me. After glancing at it for approximately a second, it vanished. "Strange, what was that?" I thought to myself and carried on with my work, which always was a very stable factor in my life: and I must humbly say, that I am thankful, that I am able to be happy whilst doing my work because otherwise, my life would be a lot emptier – I guess.

Then I started hearing branches and twigs breaking and all of a suddenly a blood-curdling scream penetrated the air. All of us were totally petrified. The scream was out of this world and Mebra, who slowly came towards me, whispered: "Careful this is a yowie and it seems to be hungry. Let us leave now. The scream, according to our tribe, is a warning sound and it usually screams, before it attacks. Come, let us drive now." I could not imagine to leave all my gear and just drive away, because of some mad animal, that most people, including me, until I was confronted with its presence, would simply deny and even mock me for mentioning it. Agony and despair commenced encumbering my soul, which really felt wretched at that moment. "Why should I go now, if this creature could even be worth a lot of money." I thought to myself. But because of another scream, which we all heard, just a minute after I had finished expressing my thoughts, which I have mentioned above, we started heading back or should I better say running back.

Fear was our companion until we reached the car and then we drove off to Rawson Village, which was south-east from where we had parked the car. The drive was quite rough and the road led us through most of the Yarra Range. After more than an hour we arrived at Rawson Village and decided to talk about the whole situation again. I decided to buy a gun and some ammo, just to be on the safe side of things. After a long talk with Mebra and Jake, I had managed to persuade them, to return with me to the place, where we had left our gear. I was absolutely convinced, that this Yowie would be there again – well it turned out totally different than I could ever even begin to envisage in my wildest dreams. What happened, you will soon read and it was quite an experience mate, as we tend to say in down under.

The moment we had arrived at the place, where we had left our gear – this time we drove up to the steep road, which led us there, for we were scared of hiking. The experience was still in our presence and it was haunting our every being. We stepped out of the car and grabbed our gear, but something was really awkward. There were things missing and I thought to myself: "What or who could have taken a part of my gear and why?"

After we had nearly finished packing everything nicely into the car, I guess it must have been around dusk, because it was getting dark and I had an eerie feeling, which I never had had before and hope not to experience again. There were still some instruments, which I took and as I put them in the car, which was parked near the place, where we had set up our camp, I could hear something wandering in the bush or should I say forest? Then I saw it in its full might – this creature. It was very big, I would say at least 4 meters or maybe even larger than that. It had fur all over its body and reddish eyes.

It came out of the bush like some figure of a vivid dream and I trembled with fear. It stared at me for at least a minute or more. This was the scariest moment of my life and I did not know what this Yowie would do to me or Jake and Membra, who were behind me and absolutely petrified. After the Yowie had totally penetrated me with its fierce eyes, it came towards me and the earth quivered by every step, that it made. It stopped right in front of me and grabbed my arm. Then the most horrid voice started speaking to me: "You leave now and if you come back and do any more research I will have you for my next supper, but don't think, that you will have a slow death. No, I will eat you alive, you dumb arrogant human! This is my last warning! Leave no with your friends – human!" The Yowie let go of my arm and simply vanished into thin air! I was in total shock and in some sort of paralysis. After a while, though I managed to regain some of my strength and will.

We hurried into the car and quickly drove off. The drive was a nightmare ride because we did not know if it maybe was lurking somewhere near the road on our way back to my hometown. Luckily nothing happened: as you can see! So, this is my story, think of it what you will, but for me, this was a mind-boggling experience, which has changed the way I perceive the world completely and I would recommend everyone, who reads this, to take this seriously. Most people just don't realize, that this creature, and probably many others likewise, are as real as you and I! So may the true light bless everyone, who reads this tale of the Yowie, which is a real entity and no myth. Hence let me finish this story with the famous quote, which I have changed a weeny bit: "Truth is really stranger than fiction!"

The End

The Yowie of Marradong

Many rumors have been heard and some tales told by aborigine tribes, mentioning a human-like beast, which they call the "Yowie". This story tells us about a farmer, who never thought, that something like this could be true until he met a creature, which was a myth or maybe probably still is a legend for most. But let me stress, that a legend has always some truths to it, or else it would not be a legend. Even if it were just the figment of my imagination, it still would have some kind validity, because this creature still would be existing in the minds of the thousands, who have perceived the "Yowie". But let me now start to present you the story of a Yowie encounter, that is maybe a bit unusual.

I am going to interview the farmer in my Perth house and let you decide, whether this account is only the figment of the farmer's imagination or the real deal. So, let me stop doing the talking and invite Mr. Dawson to tell you his own story.

It is the third of March and I am now recording this interview with Mr. Dawson.

Me: Hello Mr. Dawson it is a pleasure to have you here mate. How has your trip to Perth been?

Mr. Dawson: Fine, thanks, mate. I normally don't travel a lot, but it was a nice ride.

Me: That is nice. so maybe you can tell us a bit about you and your life?

Mr. Dawson: No problem mate. Well, I am a farmer and have been a farmer my entire life. I took over my Uncle's farm, when I was a young bloke, still quite immature, as you would tend to say it. Then I got married a few years later and took on the tradition of my being a farmer. You must understand, that my family has been farmers for at least five or six generations, so there is kind of a tradition in our family concerning that.

Me: Ok. So, when did you have your first encounter with the "Yowie" and what was it like?

Mr. Dawson: Hmmm, let me think. I guess it might have been around 1989 or so. I am not really that sure, but I would like to add something else. There were always rumors about this thing, and even my uncle and his father had been telling me, that a lot o strange stuff had been occurring in the last forty to fifty years. For instance, cattle had gone missing and some dead animals were found, which had strange marks on them. But I always doubted the existence of this creature, I never had the faintest idea, that such a thing as a Yowie could exist. I can tell you why, if you like?

Me: Well, go ahead, I am curious and I guess, that our readers are too.

Mr. Dawson: It actually is not that complicated, because I was just indoctrinated by conventional science, which normally would exclude such a cryptid. Most scientists will tell you, that such things cannot exist, for the simple reason, that there would be a lot of evidence if they did. The truth is a bit weirder than most people can even envisage because it will change your perception of reality.

I'll try to explain to you why I see it that way. The Yowie is not the only creature, which is hidden from the public view and the government knows this for a fact. The evidence, that the Yowie exists is out there if you are open-minded and ready to accept, that you have been lied to by the media and our educational system. You must comprehend, that the Yowie is not a conventional primate, it has some paranormal abilities, which would crush the materialistic fundament of mainstream science.

Me: Very interesting, so the Yowie is not only a normal creature, there is more to it than meets the eye – so to speak.

Mr. Dawson: Yeah, you are right on that one. But let me tell you something about my first encounter with the Yowie. It was a day in spring, probably the beginning of

April, to be exact the fifth of April. I was going to check some of my barns, near the road, an old road, which is not used anymore, albeit very rarely. As I was heading towards the oldest barn, I could hear something moving in the nearby bush. Then as I opened the door of my barn, I saw a figure walking at the end, the backside of the barn. The figure was very tall and bipedal. This totally shocked me, because I until then never have had any kind of out of the order experiences and this shook me to the core. Then after a while as I was inside the barn, trying to get to grips with the fact, that I had probably just seen something, that should not exist, I could hear footsteps walking around the barn and these footsteps stopped right behind me. I turned and then I saw it clearly. It was massive and hairy and had a reddish fur. The eyes had some kind of amber or yellow tone to them. The Yowie was about 50 feet, 15 meters, away from me and at least five foot or six foot taller than me, and I am a man of approximately six foot. So we are talking about a 12-foot giant, that walks upright and is able to hide and even talk, but that is another story, which I'll tell you later because it is interlinked with a later encounter. I was frozen and thought, that it might harm me, but nothing of the sort happened. The Yowie just left after a minute or so. And that was my first encounter, which I had had on the farm.

Me: That was riveting. Would you like to share some more encounters with me? I suppose, that you have had more than one?

Mr. Dawson: Yeah mate, that is true, I have had more than one. But this one was the most intriguing because it really changed a lot in my life and the way I went about it. But let me share another encounter with the yowie, which still is in some way or another a not so accepted topic in our society. About a year later, I think it must have been early spring, I was driving around my farm in the evening to check some fence poles and then suddenly about two kilometers from my farmhouse, I saw something in the reflection of my car's lights. It was a huge shadow of something big and walking upright. I stopped the car for a moment to see if it really was, what I thought it was. For some reason I did not get out of my car, which was in hindsight a good decision, for that what entailed, was odd and a bit frightening. After looking around through the windows of my car, I spotted this shadowy figure again and this time I could see, that it was hairy and bipedal. The creature differed a weeny bit from my first yowie, but it was similar in build and maybe one foot taller. This yowie had red eyes though and now I know, why it may have been reacting the way it reacted towards me. I'll touch upon this hypothesis of mine after I have finished telling you the account of this encounter.

I was amazed, that these yowies could reach such an enormous height and go unseen, or at least for most people. Then out of the blue, a rock was tossed against the back window of my car and then another one. Scared and nervous I started the motor of my car and drove off and then something really freaky happened. All of a sudden I could see the Yowie standing in the middle of the road. The Yowie must have been about 200 meters away from me. I stopped the engine again and waited patiently for it to life. To my bedazzlement, it roared and ran towards my car. I quickly restarted the engine and drove at full speed. The Yowie dodged my car and disappeared into the nearby bush. This encounter really scared the living daylights out of me and it took me a couple of days to cope with the traumata, that the yowie had inflicted upon my soul.

Me: That is very interesting and scary at the same time. You said, that you would like to talk about the reason, why you think, that the yowie was different than the other one, whom you had encountered?

Mr. Dawson: Yeah, well this yowie had red eyes and I, later through some researchers, have found out, that there are various types of yowies, which roam our great southern land. Some are friendly some are violent to deadly. The yowies with the red eyes seem to be the more aggressive kind and there are several theories for that. I actually never knew, that this topic is so complex and difficult. And by the way, there are a lot of other creatures, which cryptozoologists call "cryptids". Have you for example ever heard of the "dogman" or "mountain giants"?

Me: No, I must admit, that I have never heard of these cryptids, but it would be interesting to know more about them: but perhaps it would be better if I these creatures were to be discussed in another interview. But, please do share another encounter or more encounters with me; if that is fine with you.

Mr. Dawson: Yeah, sure mate, I can share two more encounters with you. I remember, that I had another encounter with a yowie, which was very bizarre. I'll tell you why in a second. This encounter happened about twenty years ago. It was a nice summer day and I was busy working outside, fixing an old tractor of mine. I was so into my work, that I forgot everything around me. Can you relate with these moments, when you just are living for your workmate? Well, I have had many of these moments.

This moment was of one of these. While I was repairing my tractor, I think at that point, I must have spent at least three hours or so on it, I could hear something moving in my vicinity. At first, the movements were not really loud and then they became quite audible. Suddenly I had a certain feeling, that someone or something was watching me, observing my work, like a spectator or fan his stars.

Then I heard a growl and some mumbling tones, which in my opinion are the sounds of their own language, or at least of this type of Yowie. I turned my head and there it stood with all its prowess. For a moment I didn't really know what to do or how to react, because I was utterly petrified by the presence of this being, which was huge. I personally think, that this Yowie was the biggest one, whom I have ever come across.

The Yowie had a reddish fur and yellow eyes. Its chests were very big and its shoulders very broad. I would estimate its height to be at least 13 maybe 14 foot, so that would be approximately four meters or a bit more than that. Then the Yowie, who was standing about 15 meters away from me, came a little bit towards me and yelled something, which I could not understand, but it seemed to be some sort of language; as I have mentioned before, they do have the ability to speak. I slowly stood up, not trying to lose my eye contact with the Yowie, for God knows, what it was up too.

After that, the Yowie disappeared as fast as it had appeared. But the really weird part is still to come. As I looked around my tractor, which was next to one of my barns, I could see a metal object lying in the grass. I walked towards the object and saw, that it was exactly the screw, which I needed to finish the repair of my tractor. I was stunned, for a moment or two I could not breathe, because I had come to the realization, that this Yowie meant me no harm; on the contrary, it just wanted to help me, by giving me something, which I need to finish my repair.

I would like to add, that some screws are really hard to get in my area and therefore I am really thankful, that this Yowie helped me. This signifies, that some Yowies or at least some types of Yowies are good and some are bad.

Me: This is really is a very interesting account, which implies, that not all Yowies have evil intentions, some of them or maybe many of them, are good or just want to be left alone, right?

Mr. Dawsnon: Yep, that is a correct mate and I will share another encounter with you, as I promised. This one is probably is not at all positive and I think, that the Yowie, whom I encountered, belonged to some very rare species. I had this encounter about 20 Miles from my farm. I think, that it must have been a rainy day and it was almost on the cusp of dusk. I was driving very slowly, I must have been going approximately 30 kilometers an hour or so. What I remember is, that I saw so a vague shadow of an animal walking upright. There was no shadow of doubt in my mind, that this animal was a Yowie. I am not exactly sure how tall it was, because it was moving quite fast and was walking a little hunched; but it was big, by far larger than the average human.

I think, that I stopped the car for a second and was shocked for a moment. You must know, that every time, that you see a Yowie you are a bit scared or at least in a different mental state. I guess, that it takes a while to adjust to these beings. They really are quite out of our rational and it does take a while, to get used to them. Furthermore, every encounter is different and you never know, how it is going to end, although I must say, that even the aggressive types will leave you alone if you don't provoke them.

What I would like to add is, that they seem to react to our reactions and if you keep quiet, then they will leave you alone: most of the time. This is also a reason why, I stopped my car during this encounter, shortly after I had seen it.

The Yowie noticed, that my car had stopped and appeared out of the bushes with its red eyes staring at me with some blazing emotion, which I could and cannot really decipher. Then the Yowie disappeared for a moment, only to growl and moan so loud, that it did not take me more than a second to start the car and drive away. I must have driven for a long time this night, because these growls of that Yowie, were still haunting my mind for quite some time.

The sentiments of these creatures are still an oddity to me and every time, when I happen to meet them, as I have mentioned above, they astound me.

And after this long drive, which was a hassle of its own, a turmoil of subconscious feelings of anxiety and despair, I finally managed to return to my house, where I, as I recall now, fell asleep on my couch.

And that was the last encounter, which I would like to share with you for now. Of course, I have had some more, but I believe, that they are of a different manner and could well not be directly related to the Yowie sightings on my farm. Perhaps I will share them with you another time. All the best for now!

Me: It was a pleasure having you! All the best and have a safe trip back home mate!

Mr. Dawson: Yeah, thanks mate. All the best to you too!

So, this was the interview. If you want you can ascertain further Yowie encounters, which have been reported throughout the last years. As, I always like to say at the end of something: "Check the information yourself, and take it or leave it, because in reality whether it is contrived or deceitfully construed is up to you; but maybe it is just the utter plain truth!

The End

The Werecats of Glasgow

What comes to one's mind if one touches upon the subject of were animals, which are intertwined with the topic of therianthropy. A very riveting word by the way, because it derives from two ancient Greek words: "ther" and trophein. "Ther" is the Greek word for "animal", albeit a ferocious one and trophein is a verb, which signifies to change. So, this compound of words literally means to change in an animal. But actually, it is much more than that, because this story is about a hybrid, a species half human half cat, which has been subject to some literature especially in the literature of yore, which most nowadays, of course, will enjoy to neglect and dismiss as obsolete.

Well, I am of the opinion, that the ancient accounts and stories of such beings are not at all futile, because maybe the ones, who deride these things and like to put them in the realm of fairy tales, ought to think again, because what

I am about to share with my audience, the readers of this story, is as true as any other story with some sort of credibility.

But it is clear, that the modern man, is a person of reason and logic and will always, or at least in most cases deny, that such things as a werecat can even exist because his logic tells him so. But what kind of logic, if I durst ask denies a werecat. Aren't we always amazed when we gaze up at the sky at night, which sometimes is teeming with stars and probably multiple worlds, we can't even describe, let alone understand? So, why should it not be the same with our reality? Is it not as well a complex construction of many multiple aspects, which we cannot grasp with our limited mind.

So, let me quote the famous Greek Philosopher, who said: "I know, that I know nothing." And this implies, that every world view is fallible and we should rethink our reality, because it may be just a fragment of the greater reality, just a piece of an endless mosaic, which we cannot see fully.

Hence, I must admit, that I once too thought like a man of reason and logic and came to the bitter realization, that I did not know anything, albeit only a little. Now you will know why. I don't exactly recall the day, that I passed this old house, which actually never was of any importance to me, until I discovered that It was a place, a sanctuary for a species, which has been living amongst us mere mortal boastful humans, who think, that we know it all anyway, for centuries or perhaps millennia — who can really tell?

On that day though, I really noticed that house, which had a very interesting architecture stemming from the late Romanic era, as a man was more superstitious than now and visibly more open to the realms of spiritual perception. Maybe we too could learn a lot from the monks and priests of the early middle ages, who really devoutly were following the path of spirit and true light, but to not get off on a tangent, I will now carry on with my story, so that my point can come across as an argument, which maybe could dismantle this materialistic brainwashed attitude of most men and women of science and the masses, who savor to indulge into virtual worlds of greed, bodily needs, and sports.

I guess it must have been around dusk when I drove past this house, and I ascertain, that I was looking for an antique store, which was close by. But somehow this house totally engulfed my mind and I was still thinking about it for many hours, after seeing it in full detail for the first time. Later after I had gone to the antique store, which I did find, I decided to stop my car near the house and walk for a bit. I had this sudden urge, this yearning for discovery. I cannot really explain why though because I normally am not the curious type of person, who likes to stick his nose into the affairs of others. Maybe it was the magic, the enchantment which this house exuded, that attracted me to it. So, I approached the house, which was surrounded by a beautiful garden, which was encompassed by an old metal fence.

It did not take me a long time until I realized, that the house was lit and I had the impression, that I could hear weird sound emanating from the house. At first, of course, I was not too sure and doubted it; because I, as a studied psychologist with a lot of practice in this field knew, that the mind is capable of imitating sounds, which it has once heard and created them at certain moments, especially moments of fear and doubt, which in most cases could serve as a trigger for such a form of induced sound hallucinations.

But then I was sure, that the sounds were real after I had been hearing for a few times. "What the hell is going on there." I thought and then I had the stupid idea of climbing over the fence and checking out the strange noises coming from the house. With all my strength I managed to climb over the fence, which was actually quite high, at least 7 foot or so. When I arrived on the other side the sounds stopped for a while and some mysterious energy, which I cannot describe to this day began to surround me.

I slowly started walking away from the fence towards the manor house, which must have been about 300 feet from me now. Soon I came to the realization, that I was being watched, observed by some unseen force.

Trying to overcome my fear of what would happen next, I went on until I reached the front door of the house, which was decorated by ancient symbols of old Christian and probably Greek mythology. I could see a cat-like people depicted on the walls and signs, which I could not really interpret at all because I had never come across them before.

I rang the doorbell, which was the only thing, that seemed to be the only thing about the house, which had not seen more than a century. For a minute or maybe more, nothing happened, so I decided to ring the bell again. Something I would have not done, had I known, what I was about to get into.

Then after a while, the door opened and the strangest looking creature opened the door. It was approximately 7 foot tall, perhaps a bit taller. The creature had the appearance of a human, but its body structure and its head were more like that of a catlike being. It looked at me with its green eyes and face of a yellow hide. It was hairy and I swear, that it was a bipedal cat, acting like a human and standing on two legs.

"Hello, stranger. What brings you here? May I help you? You know, you should not be wandering the streets at night, especially in this neighborhood."

the creature said.

For a moment I was in a total haze and just did not know how I should respond, but then after staring at the creature and just being taciturn, I replied trying to keep my calm: "Well, I thought, that there was some party going on, and because I am man of very curious nature and fond of adventure, I had the spontaneous idea of just calling by."

"Well, stranger. If this is so, then you can enter. But first I would like to know your name and profession stranger. This is just for security reasons, I hope you don't bother stranger." the creature responded.

"Well, I am Greg Mc Graughan and I am a psychologist, who is specialized on child-therapy," I replied. "Good, now you may enter. Come in, the party is upstairs." the creature said.

I entered and followed the strange catlike creature, listening to the door being closed by something or someone. This was one of the eeriest things, that I had experienced, although I had heard of the phenomenon of telekinesis, which I of course as a materialistically orientated psychologist denied to be true. But now I am convinced, that it is real, witnessing it myself first hand. As I continued pursuing the creature, I could hear many yells and other sounds coming from above, but not only from above, also from the doors, which were on each side of the hallway leading to the flight of stairs.

As I reached the stairs, the creature stopped and said: "Please wait here, I must talk to my Master, my Lord. I'll be back in an instant." The creature went up to the stairs and disappeared, but the sounds of laughter and weird yells, which reminded me of cats meowing.

This moment waiting for the creature was one of the uncanny moments of my life because a while after it had left, some doors opened and female looking catlike creatures exited them. They slowly walked towards me and passed me by, ascending the flight of stairs, but meowing and one even said: "Hi, stranger. Do you know what you are getting involved in? Meow!"

These words spoken by this female creature freaked me out and it took me a while to settle down my psyche.

But after that the creature, who had opened the door, returned, gently descending the stairs and said with a warm and gentle voice, which had a hideous undertone: "Please come now, the master, would like to have a word with you."

I followed it up the stairs and some inquietude was evermore encroaching my soul, which normally was of an intrepid nature, but now I was commencing to realize, that I was merely a mortal, who had really no clue, what was really occurring in this world, which really is still a great mystery to me. As I reached the hallway on the upper floor, where I could clearly hear the sounds of these beings, I felt fear, because their characters, their demeanor was not of a very noble origin. Surrounded by queer yowls, weird chortling and other noises, which I am not able to expound upon because even the thought about them makes me shiver.

Then the creature stopped in front of a large door, which must have been at least 7 feet wide and 10 foot tall. The creature knocked on the door and another creature, who looked very similar to it, opened it.

"Please enter, the master can't wait to meet you," it said and I slowly walked inside, hearing the soft slamming of the door behind me.

The room, which I entered, was a saloon and there was a desk at the end of it. Behind the desk, there were several bookshelves and a wardrobe of some sort.

Sitting behind the desk was a man with the face of a cat. He too was hairy, but his stature seemed to be of a slenderer build and his eyes were as blue as the sky on a beautiful sunny day.

"Please take a seat!" he said, pointing with at a chair, which was seated near the desk. "Guards you can leave now. I will deal with this gentleman. I would like to have a talk to him." the catlike man said.

I slowly moved to the chair and sat down. The other creatures left the room and soon I was sitting near this catlike man, without anyone in the room.

"Now. Sorry for letting you wait so long, for I have sensed your presence long before you even could fathom, that we had our party. Well, introduce yourself first and then I will tell you who I am."

the man spoke.

I trembled for a moment and then I said, trying to restrain my nervousness and my plain fear, of what was really going on. "My name is Gregor Mc Graughan and I am a psychologist, who is specialized in child therapy. I am fifty years of age and have two daughters."

"Very good, Mr. Gregor Graugahn or should I say Dr. Graughan. So, you are a psychologist, not bad. And what has urged you to trespass on my property? You know, that this an illegal act and you could be punished for this, although I must admit, that we normally punish, the ones, who transgress our rules. You must know, that we have our own society and this is the way we have survived the last centuries."

the catlike man replied.

"Well, sorry for trespassing your property. I normally don't do those kinds of things. Let's say, that my act of transgressing our law, was a mere act of curiosity and I excuse myself for doing so."

The man gave me a short glance with his startling blue eyes and then he responded: "Good, I will not punish you for now, but you will have to do something for me. By the way, I forgot to introduce myself. My name is Leonard Cathouse and I am a werecat an ailuranthrope, as you can see. I am the master of this werecat coven and today is the party for my daughter Sascha, who is a werecat too. Soon you will take part in this celebration and I want you to congratulate her to her 600th birthday. Further, I wish, that you do not share this information with anyone, albeit in a fantasy story, which most want even believe, because of their primitive indoctrinated mind. I hope, that this is clear. If you should share any of this information, which I have shared and am about to share with, you will lose everything, that you have. I hope, that this is understood."

the werecat explained.

"Of course, Mr. Leonard Cathouse. I am a man of integrity and I will not tell anyone about the things you have just told me and are about to tell me."

I said slightly intimidated by the presence of this astute werecat, which was able to read my thoughts.

"Then all is fine. And now I will go with you to the saloon, where the party is already taking place. I will hold a speech there to commemorate all the history of our proud Werecat Clan of Glasgow."

Leonard Cathouse spoke with a solemn tone in his voice.

Then Leonard Cathouse stood up and I was aware, that this werecat was humungous, taller than the other ones, which I had seen until now.

Leonard Cathouse walked with a gentle but strong stride towards the door and opened it. Then he nodded slightly and said: "Come now. I will bring you to my daughter's party." Ringing with my fears of not being able to handle this really strange situation, I managed to get up and follow him out the door and into the hallway, where he walked with such pride as if he were some sort of king, of some unknown time and age. Then he stopped at a door, where many sounds were coming from. He knocked and the door opened. This door leads to a huge saloon, where there were at least 100 or 200 Werecats, all dressed in fancy clothes and costumes. The chortling and guffawing of this werecats ceased and I passed through this crowd of werecats, following Leonard Cathouse to a lectern, where he would hold a speech. The werecats were all of the different statures and some of them even towered over Leonard House, who must at least have been over 9 foot tall.

Leonard Cathouse stepped on the lectern and took a book, which was perched on the lectern. Then he began to solemnly speak: "Dear friends, dear family. It is a pleasure to welcome you to the birthday party of my daughter, who has her 600th birthday. May her birthday be merry and hopefully the party a good one. But let me add something to commemorate the history of our coven, which has been in the City of Glasgow now for more than five hundred years since we came here from our home town of Plovdiv in Bulgaria. I hope, that you all are well and that the story of the werecats is not yet over, for we still have things to attend to, don't we? This gentleman here, who has transgressed our rules, will be put to the test, by drinking the piss of cats, which we have collected to remind us of our connection to them.

So, let us enjoy the party now and please do try the cakes and everything else; the chef, who prepared them has really recommended them. According to him, they are very delicious. Our meals are raw vegan as usual, for it has been a long time when we ate meat, which we have ceased to do, at least in my coven. So, please don't consume any animal products in my house. The last one who broke this rule was expelled and banished from this City. Now our friend will drink the cat piss in front of you, to demonstrate, that he is worthy of being a friend of our family and the werecat community. So, please Mr. Greg Graughan, would you come onto the lectern."

Now all the eyes of the werecats were fixed on me and I felt very awkward. Then I took some courage and walked to the lectern, where Leonard Cathouse stood. "Please come and stand next to me," he demanded, not losing his politeness. "Yes, Mr. Cathouse," I replied strongly abashed by this moment, which so out of this world to me. I stepped onto the lectern and stood next to this werecat giant, who was very nicely dressed by the way. "Bring us a cup of the cat piss, please," he shouted into the crowd, who was now concentrating on him. A minute later or so a gallant servant brought him the cup, elegantly making his way through the amassed crowd of now hundreds of werecats, and placed it on the desk of the lectern. "Now cheers to my daughter Griselda and all her friends. Would you please be so kind drink the cup and swear an oath of allegiance to my coven, Mr. Greg Graughan." he said and handed me the cup.

I took the cup gently and for a second I hesitated, but then seeing, that I was being observed by hundreds of werecats, who could be ferocious towards me at any instant, I decided to just drink it with one huge gulp. The horrible bitter taste of the piss stung in my pallet and I almost choked, because I could not bar its repugnant stench. I laid down the cup on the lectern and just stood, waiting for the reaction of the crowd and Leonard.

"Very good! So, let us be merry and celebrate this day of mirth. There are different rooms for every taste of music. Please ask my servants for further details. Now to you Mr.

Greg Graughan. Do you solemnly swear your allegiance to me and my coven?" Leonard Cathouse spoke.

"Yes, I solemnly swear allegiance to you and your coven." I declared earnestly.

"Fine. You may leave now and do as you wish," he replied.

After he said that he stepped down from the lectern and began to socially mingle. I stood on the lectern for some more time, observing these werecats, amusing themselves and then I decided to leave. I descended from the lectern, left the room, went down the wooden stairs and into the ancient-looking hallway, which as I now realized, was full of Leonard Cathouses family's portraits stemming from different centuries.

As I reached the door, I turned my head before I exited the manor house, to check, whether or not I was transgressing one of the werecat rules, which I then did not know about; but now I do, because Leonard Cathouse has since then been a very close friend of mine, despite him being a werecat. If I may add, I do prefer his human form which is not such an appearance compared to his werecat form. As a human, he is of a reddish-pale complexion and stands about 6 foot 7 and does not at all resemble a cat or anything of that sort.

How, he manages to cope with the fact, that he is what he is, still remains a mystery to me. And how this transmogrification works, I still haven't figured out, but I know, that I know nothing in fact.

So, this is my story and my encounter with these beings, who have indeed changed my life's perception because there are not only werecats out there yelling and partying; there is just so much more and it is true, that the night has many children and he is just one of them.

The End

The Witch

The forest was always a place, which I have feared and till recently, I did not know why, but now I know why. There have always been stories told and spread across the globe about witchcraft, which in the ancient times most men believed and even practiced. But now since the dawn of humanism and the birth of materialism, this has definitely changed. Man affirms, that in the age of reason witches cannot exist and are simply the figment of superstitious people's imagination. If this is so, why are there so many people experiencing the consequences of curses and spells?

But I am not here to argue and refute the concrete minds of most scientists – let them err and be erroneous. I don't care anymore, what they say, because they just don't know any better. How can they – if they defend a theory or better-said theories, which are their religion. But I must admit, that I also was in darkness and a godless person until I was perhaps blessed to encounter huge darkness in my life, which led me to believe in the existence of God and his abounding love for all creation.

So this is my story with a witch, whose abode was in the forest, which most locals did not dare to enter, because of her. Let me commence my experience with this witch and how I came across her. Well, the time when I had my first experience with her, was when I was already an established doctor of Psychology and working for a famous university, which I am not going to mention now, because I strongly think, that it is not of great importance in this story. I think, that it must have been around Hallows Eve or maybe after that. Everything seemed to be okay in my life, which in fact was very self-centered at that time.

But the day that Anka stepped into my life, everything was about to change. Anka was a new patient of mine, who had suffered severe trauma in her life and she told me during our many sessions, that she was being haunted by a witch in her dreams and constantly having nightmares about here and other evil beings, who were serving her.

Of course, I thought, that Anka was suffering from some dissociative post-traumatized disorder, what else should I have thought. I was just too proud to admit, that there was a lot more out there, a lot more in our self-defined reality, which I and most of my colleagues could imagine. But after recognizing, that the medicine, which I had given to her, did not work the way it should, I started to wonder in amazement, if there might be some truth to it.

So, I asked her more about the witch and where she thought, that I could find her and talk to her. Anka was not really willing at first, but after some more therapeutic sessions, she succumbed to my psychological skills and said, that she would tell me, where she lived and I was in awe, when she said, that she would live in a forest, not very far from my office. So, I decided to go with her and confront the witch. The weird thing was, that she could recognize the house, which appeared to her in her nightmares, and the house was really the way, that she had described it to me.

Hence, I knocked at the door of the house, while Anka was waiting for me in the car, which was parked out of the sight of the house, and a blond woman opened the door. The woman was quite slender in appearance and looked quite young for her age, which, as I later found out was incredible and mind-boggling. "Hello, Ms. would you mind if I could ask you some questions? I am a psychologist, who is interested in some phenomena, which cannot really easily be explained by the means of conventional science. So, is it ok with you, if I may come in for a sec." I asked.

The woman stared at me and something about her was peculiar and then she said, putting a smile on her voice: "Yes, you are welcome, come on in. My name is Trude and I am a healer. I am specialized in natural healing and am always open to help everyone." I entered the door and a strange odor pervaded the air. The entrance room of the house was quite modest, but the adjacent rooms were large and they had some sort of energy, which I cannot comprehend. The house was mostly wooden and it seemed to bear some marks of history.

The furniture and all the objects of the house seemed to be of some occult origin and I was really amazed, that someone could collect so many things, of which I could only name half of. Trude's voice interrupted my thought world and said: "Take a seat in the living room, I will bring some nice home-made tea and then we can start a nice conversation Mr. psychologist." Trude laughed, but the laugh was of some haughty or should I say arrogant nature and she was emanating something, which made me unsure of myself. There was something about Trude, that gave me the creeps, in spite of being polite and calm.

A took a seat and started glaring at the queer pictures hanging on the walls of the living room. There were some portraits as well of some women dressed in garbs of former centuries. After a while, Trude came to me and sat down on the couch, which was facing mine. "So Mr. psychologist, have you been having problems with some patients lately? Maybe one of your patients, who has been having nightmares? Well, trust me I could perhaps be of some help." she giggled. "No, everything is fine, but still there is something, that I am really interested in. These forms of healing, how do they happen? Could you explain this to me?" I replied, lying to her, because I just had that gut feeling, which turned out to be right, to not tell her, why I was seeing her. She stared at me with her gorgeous blue eyes, which had something cold about them, which I until now, have trouble putting into words.

She then explained: "Yes I can, but it is a bit complicated because there are various forms of healing someone. You must know what the patient needs, every patient has different problems and different issues. But I can tell you, what I normally do. So, are you ready, do you believe in the power of magic?" Staying calm and trying to not give off the impression, that I was agitated, I said: "I believe in what science has proven. Everything else is sheer speculation and not scientific." "Well, well, I know you scientists think, that they know it all, but I will show you something and turn you into a believer of magic. You see magic is a wonderful source, which encompasses every form of creation, coming from the source of nature itself, which is guided by a being of light.

But let me show how real magic is, are you ready?" Trude said smiling a heinous kind of smile. "Yeah, ok, please show me, I am open-minded enough to see, what you mean and maybe I can prove you to be wrong," I answered quietly. Trude gave me a wink and told me to follow her into her cellar, which was at the back of her big house. We went down a set of stairs, which were in some storage room of some sort. Going down the stairs, gave me a feeling of unease. The cellar was really awkward and I could feel something bad there, which started to protrude my mind, because I always had denied evil, and even during my many sessions, had tried to explain it with psychological methods and simply said, that it was just perpetrated by people who were mentally ill. But now I know, that I was very naïve, because illness and evil are not the same, although they might coincide in some cases.

Trude led me through the rooms of the cellar until we came to some sort of well. Next to the well was a cauldron, a black big caldron. The caldron was boiling and had some weird substance in it. The color of this substance was pink, with some shades of greyish black.

Trude took a cup out of a shelf, which was on the wall next to the cauldron and filled it up with some of the substance, with which the cauldron was full of. Then she mumbled something, which I did not understand. "Now we will go upstairs again and I will show you some of the powers of magic," she said giggling again, but this giggle was haughtier and could have had some demonic attribute to it. So, I followed her again upstairs and we ended up in her kitchen, which also was of great interest to me because I had never seen so many utensils. There were all kinds of herbs, you name the herb, she probably would have had it. I watched her taking some herbs, which she then gently through inside the cup. Then she stirred the cup and started mumbling again in some strange idiom, which I could not recognize, let alone understand. It was very eerie and the whole process of slowly sprinkling the herbs on to the substance was very disturbing for me to witness.

"Here it is my special concoction, which I have just finished and blessed with the power of the Lord of nature and the realms above. Would you like to try some of it? You just have to take a sip and then you will experience something, which you probably have never experienced?" she said whilst smirking. "I don't know, I am not so sure whether I should try it or not?" I responded slightly with the disease. "Come on, just take a sip, everything will be fine, it is just a nice potion. It is an old recipe from my grandmother, just try some of it!" Trude said in a persuasive tone. I am not really aware until this day, how Trude managed to persuade me, but she did and then I replied: "Okay, I'll drink some of the potions." Trude took a cup off one of her many kitchen shelves and poured some of the potions into it. I took the cup and said: "Thank you very much." After having said that, I at first just sipped some of the potions and then drank all of, what was remaining in the cup. Soon thereafter I felt dizzy and something commenced to enshroud my mind, which seemed to be in some kind of haze, which I could not really describe, let alone comprehend. Trude burst into laughter and it echoed through the whole house. Suddenly Trude turned into something else and strange creatures surrounded her and the house, as I perked out the window of her kitchen. It was ghastly. "You fool, don't you know, that I am not aware of who you are? I know, why you have come here and I could feel, that you are trying to help this girl, who is destined to be a sacrifice for my Lord, the father of nature. Come my Lord Pan and show this mere mortal, who you are and what power magic really has." Trude shouted. Trudes face began to spin around me and I could see, that it transformed into the face of an old woman covered with wrinkles and scars. Her blue eyes took on a shade of grey and there was some reddish light exuding from them. I felt more and tipsier and swerved around the kitchen until I finally fell on the floor. Then I was totally concealed by some form of murky darkness, which I had never experienced before in my life.

But I remember waking up in a bed inside a little hut. The door of the hut was open and a cold wind was blowing. Moments after waking up I could see, as I looked out of the opened door of the hut, the image of a dark and tall creature, which had the appearance of a dragon, not very far from where my bed was standing next to a fire, which was burning a few hundred feet away from the hut. A woman, who must have been Trude, was dancing naked around the fire and chanting in a very intimidating language, which made me shudder. Her chanting included some yells and vociferating screams, which were of such an evil nature, that caused me to despair. Full of anxiety and unease I decided to get out of that bed and flee.

As I came out of the hut though, this being, this tall dark figure instantly appeared in front of me and paralyzed me. Then it levitated my whole body and thrust me right next to that bonfire. The woman stopped chanting and then yelled at me: "Now you will bow down to my master and tell me where the girl is hiding, you ludicrous scum. I am the witch of this forest and my master is yearning for another corban, do you understand. Hahaha." "Why should I bow to anyone, I don't believe in this stuff, magic is just a figment of our human imagination, there are no such things as witches. You are a sick and deluded person, if you really believe in the things, which you are saying. You need psychiatric help; by the way, I know some good psychiatrists, whom you could visit." I uttered, trying to manipulate her in some way: because to tell you the truth, I was extremely scared and trembling. After I had said that Trude glared at me and penetrated my soul with her evil eyes and then the whole forest was lit up with a bluish light, which had a darkish hue to it. "Lord of Darkness and Light, come down! I am your humble servant.

Give me your power so I can atone for the trespasses, caused by this ignorant psychologist. Come to me now o Lord of Darkness." Trude muttered loudly. Shortly after she had uttered these words, which were very vile and cruel, a huge figure appeared, which had a light consisting of shades of grey and blue. The figure spoke in a clear but cold voice: "Very good, sacrifice is always welcome to me. Who shall it be? O, this man here, well you know what to do witch!" Kill him, and drain him of his blood!" I was startled and did not know how I should react, every second was pain and anguish and I thought, that I would die any second from now on.

The tall dark figure grabbed me and began to drag me through the forest, while the witch was hovering in the air, watching me and her surroundings. I don't know, how long I was being dragged through the forest, but I realized, that the tall dark figure had come to a halt and then again I heard the voice of Trude: "We are close to the altar, but I will sacrifice him her and bring his dead corpse to it. Tie his hands and legs and prepare everything for the ceremony, I will wait here." The tall dark figure quickly appeared next to me and bound my hands and legs with two metal chains, which it wound multiple times around my hands and legs, locked with two silver locks and vanished. Now I was left with Trude, looking out on a meadow, which spread out in front of me. We had arrived at the other end of the forest, which in fact is many miles wide and long. Trude stared at me with her sinister sparkling eyes and now I could see how evil she was.

This woman was a real witch and I don't even know how long she already had been dwelling on this earth, but soon I would find that out. For sure she was very old because I could feel her wisdom and her aura now, which could augur, that she was not a normal mortal, although she did not look very old. "See, magic is real and you are my next sacrifice! I have been the witch of this forest since the early settlers have set foot on this land. I have seen kingdoms rise and fall. I am a great witch by the way and I was born more than two thousand years ago. You stupid human, do you really think, that you could thwart my plans? Tamper with my affairs, no-no?" she chuckled. Then she started mumbling something in an idiom, which I could not understand, but I could tell, that it was not the same idiom, which she had been babbling in the kitchen, that was sure. But if she was that old, how many languages did she know?

Maybe she was able to speak hundreds of languages, which would not astound me at all, considering the fact, that some human beings even manage to apprehend up to a hundred or more tongues in a short life span, how many could someone like her, with her evil powers, be able to learn? But, this was not what shocked me the most, it was her person and the traits of her character, which vexed me, and were an abomination to me and the creator, whom I have come to know in the meanwhile. After about half an hour or so the tall dark figure reappeared next to her. But then something amazing happened. As Trude and the tall dark figure were conversing in yet another very strange language, I could see a light in the distance, which was coming closer and closer to me.

After a while, Trude seemed to have finished the conversation with the tall murky figure. She came towards me again and was holding a dagger or maybe a kriss, in her hands, I am not absolutely sure, because the light of the moon did not directly shine on the spot, where I was lying. She halted facing downwards onto my head. The moment she knelt down and stabbed me with the weapon in the stomach.

The first stab was painful and gave me the impression as I had plunged into a pool of a million needles. Then swung the weapon again and stabbed my left leg and then my right one. Finally, as she was about to stab me in the neck, I heard a loud voice yelling: "I rebuke you in the name of

Yeshua Cha Massiah you wicked witch. I bind your powers in the precious blood of the lamb."

Trude was perturbed for an instant, but then she tried to stab me, but some force pushed the weapon away from me. Cross and full of rage she stood up and screamed: "Servants of darkness kill this imbecile of a priest!" The tall dark figure and some other creatures, which I could not really identify, cam hurrying towards the big source of light, which was a priest an angel and girl. "By the power of God, by the might of Yeshua I expel you from this forest, you beings of evil." the priest yelled.

The beings were trying to assault the priest and the girl, but the light seemed to always hurl them back. After a while, the beings gave up and dissolved from one instance to the next. Trude stood up and attacked the priest and the girl with some kind of spell, which was not tangible for me.

"By the power of all darkness, I curse you! Die now you ludicrous priest. Anka, you traitor, you will perish now too!" Trude screamed with all her might.

The priest and Anka were suddenly engulfed by some very dark mist, but after some time had passed the darkness surrounding them faded away and Trude cast another spell, but this time it did not work at all and Trude was thrown back at least 60 feet by an unseen force. Groaning and whining she left muttering: "I'll be back, I am the witch of this forest. I am and I will find a way to defeat you."

Then there was silence and the light soon thereafter had arrived at the place, where I was lying. I cannot recall exactly what happened, I only know, that the priest and

Anka had somehow gotten me out of the forest and brought me home. As I woke up the next morning, I found out to my great amazement, that my wounds had been healed and the priest, whose name was George, was standing next to my bed with Anka. "It is over. I will take care of Anka now. Don't worry about the witch, she has abandoned her home and will hopefully never again be seen in the forest. I will pray with some colleagues over the witch's house and the forest. The prayers should ward her off. Probably she has already found some new abode and other potential victims. Sadly, we cannot track her, because her identity is false. But the real good news is that we have found the bones of dead people in her house: dead people, who have been missing for quite some time. So, I am sure, that she will not come back in a while." George said with a comforting voice and left my bedroom. Anka still stayed for a short moment and then spoke to me with a soft voice: "Thank you so much for risking your life to help me. We'll keep in touch. Bye." Anka left my bedroom and me to my own devices.

So, this is the end of my personal experience with a witch. So please bear in mind, that many things exist, which we cannot understand, and I presume, that there are many other witches out there, albeit not of the same sort as Trude.

The world really is strange, definitely a lot stranger than fiction.

The End

The Vampire Hunter

It is another cold and grey day in a humungous concrete jungle, which civilized man calls a „city", but I ascertain, that a „city" is just a pit hole, a huge mess of many tragedies, that even the most sensitive, cannot really grasp. For me, though this day is a special day, for I have finally found, what I am looking for and have been tracking down for a long time. I don't know for how many years, because I don't keep track of what exactly, but I know, that my reward will be great and the council is waiting for me to accomplish my mission.

Until now I have bickered with the hardest hardships, which man can face and I am not wanting to let down the council. Justice will have to be done and I am a hunter, who has sworn allegiance to the council, which has been loyal to me ever since I am, what I am. Too long this vampire has broken the rules and now he will be put to justice by me. Luckily, I can smell their scent and am blessed with a lot of experience.

Why this is so, you might ask now? Well, that is my secret, that I will reveal to you at the end of my story. This story is a bit out of the ordinary compared to my other experiences, that I have made as a hunter. Normally it is easy and not such a hard task to find a vampire, who has committed crimes against the council and its rules. These sorts of vampires are renegades, outcasts and they are mostly alone, and therefore quite easy to hunt and defeat, but this one is not, because this one is a very old and strong one, who has a high rank and a whole coven on its side. And I must admit, that this vampire is the first vampire lord, who I am hunting. I don't even know at times, if I am worthy of this job, because I don't know if I am capable of defeating such a strong opponent, who has hundreds of vampires on his side.

This is probably why I have been studying him for so long, waiting until he goes somewhere, where he is not well protected, but even then, he is surely a big challenge, because he has been around for a very long time, and if I say very long, I normally mean it. So now I am here waiting for this lord to go out and I hope, that my informant has lured him successfully out of his coven!

By the way, I believe in the true light, although I myself am a vampire because I have seen it and the true light of God has given me so much grace throughout the ages! Why should a vampire-like me not be able to believe? I know, that some will judge me for saying this, but who is there to judge me? Only God can judge and not you mere mortals! But let me carry on with the story, which is about to become exciting, because I never thought, that this day would be a real showdown and I did not expect, the things, which would happen! So now I will tell, what occurred, when I was walking down the street with a lot of sun cream on my face and a good light jacket, protecting me from the light of the sun. I was heading for a café, where my contact wanted to meet up with me. He had just called me, quite concerned about the latest happenings and he was convinced, that this vampire lord called Rufus, would be at a theatre around 6 to 7 p.m.

As I was strolling towards the café I noticed, that someone was following me, at first I thought, that I might already be suffering from some sort of paranoia, which I could have gotten, in retrospective to all the experiences, that I had had the last 10 to 20 years, I took it into account, but then my senses, which are usually very sharp, told me, that there were vampires out there watching me. At that time, I didn't know, what was going, but I was already sure, that at least 3 or four vampires were on my tail, and they were not council vampires, because these had another sort of scent and aura.

Realizing this made me a bit anxious, and I watched my every step. Time passed and the cafe was already insight, and I had an idea, how to distract these spies or guards, who were watching the area, trying to find out, who or what I was. So I waited a while in a store about one block from the café. The store was some sort of Deli and I stayed there, buying some weird coffee and sat down on a plastic chair next to a vending machine. I took out a newspaper, which I had just brought from a newspaper shop and started reading it. I think, that my ruse worked, for two very tall and pale guys entered the store.

They wore black jackets and looked like the typical gothic, but something about them, revealed, that they were vampires, probably working for Rufus. They looked around the store and spotted me, then one of them passed me and asked me: „Excuse me, Sir, could you please tell me what time it is?" I was a bit bewildered, as he asked me this superficial question, which was a trick to lure me into a trap. I kept very calm, looked at my watch and said: „It is exactly five forty five." The guy looked at me and I discovered, that he had a symbol, which meant, that he was a guard of Rufus and replied briefly: „Thank you, sir. Very kind of you!" Then he and the guy left the store and I knew, that I would have to leave out the backway of the store, which leads into a courtyard.

But I was amazed as I saw these guys again and I knew, that they weren't there for a nice talk. One guy approached me and asked me: „Excuse me sir, but I think that you have lost something, here it is!" I looked at him and then he made a sudden frown and grabbed my arm, whilst drawing out a sword with his other arm. "No, I don't think so. But I know, why you are here." I said and pushed him aside. The other guy was now standing right behind me and said: "Ready to die, hunter? We've been waiting."

"Not without a fight," I replied and jumped over him. Then the fight started, which ended badly for them because the underestimated my subtle reaction and my speed. In no time they were done with and their bodies headless. I know, that this may sound cruel, but it was either their life or mine. And I am a hunter, who is paid to do his job, that is the way it works, even if the council will normally take care of executing some vampire, who did not abide by the rules, there are still many, who won't or cannot be captured easily.

Although I admit, that in most cases I just tranquilize them with some special bullets, but sadly I cannot always avoid a deadly battle. This I am not saying to justify my actions, for I know, that they may be wrong, but should one let vampires break their own laws and kill innocent, or at least poor humans on their own will and for their own pleasure?

Well, I don't think so, this is why hunters like me exist, this is why the council is counting on hunters like me. But now I would like to continue with my story because it doesn't end here and before I found this vampire lord, I still had to do some more research. I can also tell you why, simply, for one reason: he somehow noticed, that I had been tracking him down and left the city and hid in some old mansion, which was very well guarded by the way.

The two guards or should I better call them the vampire Lords henchmen. I got the heads and the dead bodies and dragged them into the corner of the courtyard. Then I sliced them into chunks and threw them in the next container, what I normally did, so this was a usual procedure, even if it was not so comfortable for me, but this only happened when I had no other option. After that, I went out on the street again and met up with my contact, who told me, that this vampire lord was out of the city and hiding in some mansion, where he was well guarded. This, of course, was a new situation for me, so I decided to contact the council and tell them, that I would need some assistance, because I did not want to risk my life, trying to kill dozens of vampires, just to get to a lord, who powers I could not estimate.

As I informed the council the next day, they seemed to understand the situation and said, that they would come with me, to deal with the situation, because they did not want their world to be revealed by some curious detective, who would not stop investigating, until he found out about us.

So the council told me, to wait a while near the mansion and listen to their further instructions while checking out the area. Well, that is what I did and started walking around the town of Maynard and stayed at a place (another contact's place) near the beautiful Assabet River, which was actually quite charming at night. During the day I slept in a coffin and sometimes I would watch stupid tv shows, trying to clear my mind and preparing myself for a potential battle, which may even have a bad outcome for the council. I tried to use the time, to find out as much information about the mansion as I could and the possible connection, which Rufus could have with it. What I found out was amazing.

First of all the mansion was built in the late eighteenth century and it was used by some strange coven for practicing the dark arts. "Interesting stuff." I thought to myself, whilst reading about the accounts of the mansion. "Why was Rufus there and did he have any connection with this coven? Was the coven still existing? I couldn't find any evidence, that it still was, but who really knows?" I pondered and tried to maintain my patience because it was really hard to be patient these days with a guy like Rufus on the loose, who could have ties with all sorts of people or creatures of the night, which are not only vampires.

I am just stating that, because some may just associate us with this term, but you are wrong, there are actually multitudes of species running around and you humans, just don't know and most of the time don't care. Well, that is all in all another story. But I would like to mention some experiences, which I had before I entered the mansion with the council and its little private vampire army. I must admit though, that the battle itself may not have been so spectacular, but the things which happened before might have been. One night, while I was wandering along the Assabet River and delving into my thoughtworld, I could sense someone following me and then I decided to follow him, by camouflaging myself with a mental trick, which works most of the time.

This, someone, happened to be a Satanist and a member of that coven, which had a meeting that night in some old house. I watched the house, which was illuminated in a strange way, from a good distance. I was really in awe, as I saw, that some demon seemed to appear in the midst of at least 10 or 15 Satanists, as I peeked through one of the windows. I had seen rituals of this sort before, but I still was astounded, that they were taking place in this day and age in a manor house, which was not very far from the mansion, where Rufus was staying.

Then there was another strange occurrence, which I would like to mention, it occurred a day or two before I would confront Rufus with the council. I was wandering again along Assabet River as I could hear loud thumping noises, which definitely were coming from the nearby bushes. At first, I ignored them, but then I could perceive a shadowy figure of a huge doglike creature walking in a bipedal manner. The creature snarled and seemed to snort. I was a little anxious at first and then I realized, that this coven had either summoned a werewolf or mastered the art of therianthropy.

This creature glanced at me and then it started howling. The eyes of this werewolf were amber and vicious vibes were emanating from it. The werewolf charged at me and I knew, what I had to do. I pulled my gun, which I had with me and fired all the rounds, then I jumped aside, and its right hand's claws almost ripped me apart. I then took my sword out of its sheath.

The werewolf charged again and this time, it was right on me, trying to bite me. I held my sword in front of my head and pushed it back with all my might. This werewolf was strong, but could it keep up with my celerity? I leaped back and then waited for it to charge again. It ran towards me and I dodged before it reached me and then hit it with my sword with all my strength. The werewolf screamed and charged again. I dodged its attack again and pierced a part of its stomach with my sword twice. I was really hitting it fast, so fast, that it could not react. But this werewolf was very resilient and it attacked me until I finally managed to cut off one of its arms. Then it vanished. "That was close," I recall, saying, after that battle, which could have taken 10 minutes or more. But now I knew, that I would have to inform the council right away.

A werewolf in this area, and probably a Satanist transformed into one was a serious matter, which should be dealt with, and that is why I called the council right away. Sadly I could not contact them that night, but they called me early in the morning. I told them, that I was almost killed by a werewolf creature, which had an unknown origin. This changed things for the better, because, they promised to send some aid to me and observe the area.

And this is what happened. The council sent in some vampires to observe every house in the area at night. I remember, that shortly before I met the council near the mansion, where Rufus was hiding, that these vampires told me, that they had not only seen werewolves but other weird wereanimals and monsters. They also said, that they were feeling a bit uneasy about these things going on and did not want full-blown war with this coven, which seemed to have some connection with these creatures. "I understand, you don't want a war, because you don't want the people to know about us and our society. I can understand these guys, but these monsters are endangering human lives and maybe even ours. We have to take care of the matter and you have to inform the secret council because this could be a very urgent matter!" I said to the 20 vampires, who were listening to me at an old graveyard, where we met before I would go to Rufus with the council. "Of course, we will inform the secret council, and have them analyze the situation. Good, then stay at my place. I'll be going to Rufus with the council now. If anything strange happens, please call me!" I replied. "Good, we will do that and kind of try to reassert the things we have observed!" one of the vampires said, I think he is called Jack or Jacob. I had only seen him a few times, and sadly I cannot remember his name.

But that is not important now, because I am about to share the rest of this story with you. I left the graveyard, which was a few miles away and got into a car, which I had leased for some time. I drove to the beginning of the road, which leads to the mansion, and was perhaps only a few hundred yards from the mansion.

It was dusk or at least almost dusk, as far as I can vividly remember because my meeting with the vampires at the graveyard was around 4 p. m. or so. I forgot to mention something else, before I tell you, what happened at the mansion because the secret council is not a normal council. It is a higher more powerful form of our society's political instance and way more secretive, than the normal council, which is known by most vampires by the way — the secret one is not, and there is a reason for that, but that is in all a different story.

Before the council arrived, I decided to take a better look at the mansion and strolled around its gates a bit. There were vampires there and a strange scarecrow-like figure, which really gave me a great sense of unease. The figure was very tall and of slender stature. Its eyes had something demonic or plain evil in them and I cannot tell you what it was, but I think it must have been its essence.

To be honest with you I have never seen such a creature and it stared at me for a moment and gave me the feeling as if it could read me like an open book. Then it disappeared into the mansion with some guards. It became dark and I got a call from the council. "We will be arriving soon with 10 vans. Please wait near the mansion, but don't go inside. It might be too dangerous. If Rufus should try to resist us or manage to kill one of us, which is unlikely, then the secret council will take care of him." a council member told me on my cell phone. Time passed and then 20 black vans arrived. There were five council members, who approached me, as they stepped out the first van. I guess, there must have been at least 200 or more vampires with them. They all had guns, with special ammunition and crossbows. A council member, who was the eldest of the five started talking to me: "My dear hunter, we will now get Rufus alive or dead, for he has already caused enough trouble in this world. We will now open the gates of the mansion and you will follow us, but don't say a word. We will do the talking." "Ok!" I answered.

We went to the gate of the mansion and rang the doorbell at least 10 times. Nobody answered so the council members decided to break the lock of the gate. They even had a locksmith to do that and it only took them a few minutes. Then we entered the property and I could feel evil pervading the atmosphere surrounding the mansion and the property. We came to the huge door of the mansion and knocked at the door many times. We waited for a while and then the eldest of the council got someone to pry the door open. Which took some moments.

The door cracked open and fell onto the ground. The council members went inside and I followed. "Rufus we are here to bring you to justice! Come with us!" the members cried, while I was analyzing the situation. The mansion was big and there was a staircase leading up. We went upstairs and the 200 Vampires or so stormed inside the mansion, checking ever room at the ground floor. Upstairs we could perceive some strange sounds and we checked every room until we stumbled across a door, which was locked. "Pry it open." the eldest of the council members said to the locksmith, who was behind me. After a minute or so the door was open and what we saw was terrifying. There was a huge saloon, where Satanists and this scarecrow figure, who reminded me of this creature in the movie "Jeepers Creepers" feeding of a corpse, which looked like Rufus. "Stop what you are doing, you are surrounded!" the council members screamed!

The Satanists stared at us and attacked us viciously with their magic, but they were no match for the council because they fired their guns, which were loaded with bullets of light. The Satanists fell to the ground and were dead, but that creature just kept attacking the council and tore on of it's members to shreds! I took my sword and told the locksmith to get all the vampires upstairs because this creature was turning out to be a great threat.

The creature tried to attack me, but I dodged its attacks and managed to slice off one of its arms. Then it stared at me with its evil eyes and ran to the window at the end of the saloon and jumped through it as if it were thin air! Now the saloon was filled with many vampires and I could hear shots coming from outside. Then it was silent again and I have never ever heard or seen of it again. "It's over, Rufus is dead, we are done here. Get rid of the dead bodies and clean up the place." the eldest of the council told one of the vampires. "Of course sir!"

So this was it. This is one of my stories, and to tell you the truth: the weirdest one. I am glad, that I have not had another encounter with such a creature. Whatever it was, it probably had some connection with the Satanists and could have easily killed Rufus. I have never seen such might and strength, and believe me, I am not a weak foe, and have had my share of strong opponents, but this was just totally out of this and my world.

Hope to have informed you well and wish you all the best. May God bless you, who- or whatever you are.

The End

Printed in Great Britain
by Amazon